THESE HAUNTED HILLS

HILLS

A COLLECTION OF SHORT STORIES

Linda Hudson Hoagland (2)

Jan-Carol Publishing, Inc
"every story needs a book"

These Haunted Hills
A Collection of Short Stories

Published September 2017
Mountain Girl Press
Imprint of Jan-Carol Publishing, Inc
Copyright © 2017 These Haunted Hills
ISBN: 978-1-945619-38-0
Library of Congress Control Number: 2017956021

You may contact the publisher:
Jan-Carol Publishing, Inc.
PO Box 701
Johnson City, TN 37605
publisher@jancarolpublishing.com
jancarolpublishing.com

This is dedicated to all the talented authors for their participation in this collection of short stories, and to all the readers of Jan-Carol Publishing's books.

Table Of Contents

THE DEVIL
BEHIND THE BARN

JAN HOWERY

During the 1800s, farm life was hard. James Wilson Morgan knew this all too well.

James Wilson Morgan, nicknamed JW, was born into a large Bible-believing, cattle-raising family in rural Southwest Virginia. The family farm was over 1000 acres, with cattle, horses, chickens, goats, and most every other farm animal—other critters, too. At the early age of eighteen, JW married his childhood sweetheart, Jane, who was only sixteen. He and his new bride moved into an old farmhouse with an old barn on the land that his father deeded to them as a wedding gift. The farmhouse had been vacant for a long time, and needed some fixing up. The barn was in need of repairs, too.

Life was not easy. Five years later, Jane was a mother of twins—one of each, a boy and a girl—and was expecting another baby. JW worked on the farm, cutting timber to clear the land, building more barns for more cows, and laboring in the fields from early morning until late night. Jane worked in her home, as any woman did in the 1800s. She worked in her vegetable garden, prepared meals for her family and the hired farm workers, tended to all the chores of the housekeeping, and much more.

JW decided one Saturday night that he was going into town with a

1

couple of his hired farm hands. He told Jane it was because he wanted to be sure that the hired hands didn't get into trouble. After three months of JW disappearing every Saturday night to the local bar and dragging himself home at the wee hours of Sunday morning, Jane decided she'd had enough of his rowdy, irresponsible, non-husband like behavior.

"It is Sunday, and you are goin' to church with me this mornin'. You were out all night? Well, you should have thought about church before you stayed out all night drinkin' with your buddies. Get the horse and buggy. We are goin' to church," Jane said sternly, as she dressed the children.

"If you wanna go to church, go on. You can walk. I'm too tired. Besides, I'm still drunk. We boys just had a little innocent fun. I need it. I work from daylight to dark, and I have to cut loose once in a while," JW snapped.

"You've been cuttin' loose for three months now! The baby is on the way, and I have cooked, cleaned, had your young'uns, worked in the garden, carried in the wood for the cookin' stove, and I have everything else to do around this house. I'm tired too! JW, I need a husband. You are not one of the work hands. You are my husband," Jane said fighting back the tears.

"Old woman, I am not goin' to church with you!" JW yelled.

"Old woman? I am not your 'old woman,' old man!" Jane screamed. "Now look what you've done! You got the young'uns cryin'! Your yellin' got 'em upset."

"Well, if you would just go and leave! Get out of here! Leave me alone!" JW demanded.

"I am not goin' anywhere! Your mother and father always want to know where you are on Sundays. What am I to tell 'em? I'm tired of it! If you can't go, I will just stay right here and you can listen to your young'uns squallin'!" Jane snapped.

JW turned around and with an open hand, slapped Jane's face. The astonishment of what just happen caused time to freeze. The children stopped crying and Jane stood in shock. JW had never raised his hand to her. He had always been kind and gentle, and very loving. Since he had been staying out with the 'boys,' his temperament had changed. He had changed. He was bitter. He was angry. He was always in a bad mood.

When Jane finally caught her breath, she took a step backward, turned, and walked away without a word or a tear. She was numb. The two little ones followed her into the kitchen.

JW was as shocked as anyone. *What the hell did I just do?* he thought. *I never should have hit her. But damn it, I have had it. She is always on my ass to do something!* JW picked up his coat, stormed out the front door, and slammed it shut. He searched the pocket of his coat for his bottle of whiskey. *Yes! There it is,* he thought. He took a big swig of whiskey and stomped up the hill along the dirt path to the barn.

The barn was very old, and had shown every one of its years when they moved to the farm. It was up on top of a hill, not far from the house. JW had done repairs on the barn, and he was proud of his work. The originally falling-down barn was now a big structure, with twenty cattle milking stalls, feeding troughs, and two large hay lofts. Wooden doors were built into both sides of the barn for herding the cows through. Hay and straw cushioned the floors.

"Well, I am not going to take it any longer!" JW said out loud to himself. "I want to do things and go places. I am not going to let some woman tell me what I can or can't do!" He reached for the wooden barn door handle, pausing when he heard a rustling noise from behind the barn. *What was that?* he thought. He stood for a moment, listening for the sound again. *Nothing.* As he reached for the handle again, the rustling noise grew louder. *Did that old bull get out again? Guess he's like me! He's got places to go,* JW thought and smiled to himself.

JW took another swig of whiskey and put it back in his pocket, then walked around the corner of the barn. As he rounded the corner, JW saw an upside-down bucket. *Where did that come from?* he thought. He walked over to the bucket, picked it up, and looked at the ground under it. He examined the bucket, then put it back down, flipped over, and sat on top of it. He fished the whiskey bottle out of his pocket and took another swig. As he swallowed hard, JW smelled something burning. This time, the rustling sound was deafening; it was coming from the bucket.

JW jumped up as if his pants were on fire, kicking the bucket into the air as his whiskey bottle dropped to the ground. As the bucket fell from high in the air back to the grass, JW couldn't believe his eyes. When the bucket hit the ground, he blinked, rubbed his eyes, and felt nauseated by the smell of burning flesh. It was undeniable; JW was eyeball to eyeball with the devil himself. The devil stood almost seven feet tall, with red parched burnt flesh, two pointed ears, burning eyes, a long dragon-like tail, broken teeth, and a shining pitchfork in his claw-tipped hands.

"I am here to take you places you want to go," growled the devil. "You will see things that you have never seen before." The devil's words rang with an evil delight.

JW was paralyzed with fear. He was face to face with evil. His whole life, as short as it was, flashed before his eyes—but it was the future he saw afterward that he didn't want to see. He saw his children growing up without him, his loving wife married to another man, and his parents missing him. Yes, he was going places, all right; he saw it was an eternal pathway of destruction.

The devil let out a burst of haunting laughter, and took a big gulp from JW's whiskey bottle. The evil laughter snapped JW back to the reality of his situation. He could move again. He turned and ran like the wind of unharnessed tornado. He looked back as he rounded the corner of the barn to see the devil was closing in on him, with the pitchfork only inches from his behind. Still running, JW looked toward the farmhouse and yelled, "Jane! Jane, I need you! Help! Help me! Please!"

Jane, sitting in the kitchen, was surprised when she heard JW yelling. It sounded like he was in pain. *He's bein' hurt*, she thought. She ran out the back door yelling, "JW, what's wrong? What's happenin'? I'm a-comin'!"

As the back door slapped shut behind her, she saw JW was already standing in the backyard. He was so out of breath that he couldn't speak. "What happened to you? You look like you've seen a ghost!" Jane asked.

"I just...want you to...know...that we...are goin' to go to church...every Sunday. And...no more Saturday nights with the boys... Jane...I will never hit you again. I am so sorry. The only place I want to go is wherever you go," JW humbly said between gasping breaths.

"What has happened to you, JW? What on earth changed your mind?" Jane asked.

Looking up the hill toward the barn, JW said with conviction, "It was the devil behind the barn."

JW and Jane lived happily ever after.

ESTHER ON YOUR BACK

KATIE MEADE

High upon a mountain in the hills of Southwest Virginia in a place called High Knob, there is a tale that has been part of the mountain heritage for many decades. Mountain people swear this tale is true; some vow that they have experienced Esther's ride first hand. People who live in the mountains of High Knob say that you can't cross the bridge leading up into the mountains (which has become known as Esther's bridge) after dark, if you don't want Esther on your back.

You see, Esther was a young woman who got lost in the mountains of High Knob many years ago while going for a walk on a warm spring day. People looked for Esther for days, but could not find her. Not one of the people in the community where Esther lived thought she would ever walk into the mountains so far, but she did. That innocent walk resulted in Esther meeting her demise.

Esther left home on that sunny day planning on picking wild flowers and watching the rabbits, birds, and squirrels. Esther thought perhaps she might even encounter a deer, or possibly see a bear. Who knows what she experienced on that faithful day, before she started out of the mountain to find her way home? However, one thing is for sure; Esther never returned from her walk in the mountains. The reason why she never made it back

5

home is still not known. Most people who lived in Esther's community believed that she walked too far into the mountains and got lost after darkness fell upon her.

Spring rain started to fall the day Esther got lost. The rain fell in sheets, eventually causing creeks and rivers to rise to flood levels. Esther had no warm clothing, food, or water, so she just wanted to get home as soon as possible. Trying to find her way out of the mountains, Esther dared to cross a small footbridge that had flood water running over it. Darkness had already fallen in the mountains, so she could barely feel the bridge under her feet. As fate would tell, Esther should have stayed in the woods. Just as she reached the middle of the bridge, the rushing water carried her away. Esther's body was never recovered. The only evidence of her demise was pieces of torn clothing along the creek.

Decades later, the story of Esther and her infamous ride across the bridge in the mountains had been told time and time again by people who insisted that they had experienced Esther's ghostly ride across the bridge in the mountains. The legend goes that anyone who dares to cross the bridge where Esther lost her life after dark risks having Esther jump on their back, and ride them to the safety of the ground on the other side of the bridge. A young man named Doyle Shell learned about Esther's ride in a very terrifying and personal way.

During the autumn days of mountain life in 1947, the weather began to change, bringing cooler nights and days that served as a welcome relief for the mountain community of High Knob. Fall had gradually eased its usual appearance into the community where Esther had lived decades earlier, located in the mountains of Virginia. Beautiful leaves carpeted the ground once again, making individuals take to the woods for different reasons. Men of the community were not as interested in the beauty as they were the hunting season for squirrel and deer. Gathering flowers and nuts could be left to the women, as far as the men were concerned.

The harvest was completed, and people were enjoying the bounty of their labor in the community where Doyle and his good friend Donald lived. Most of the people who lived in this mountain community were farmers or coal miners. People there relied heavily on the crops and livestock that they raised, along with the wild game abundant in the mountains, to survive during the winter months. This was the very season that

Doyle looked forward to. He took pride in the large number of squirrels he brought home every fall. This year was even more exciting, because Doyle had a new friend who had moved into the community to hunt with him—or at least Doyle thought he did.

One warm fall day, Doyle got out of bed in the mood to go hunting. He wanted to go on a hunting trip to celebrate the new rifle he had rewarded himself with, after the crops were harvested. He was soon on his way to see if his friend Donald wanted to go squirrel hunting with him. Hunting alone was never as much fun as hunting with a friend, especially your best friend.

Doyle found Donald sitting at the breakfast table when arrived at the house where Donald lived with his parents. "Howdy Doyle. Come on in and have a bite of breakfast," Donald greeted him.

"Don't mind if I do," Doyle said. "It's been a few minutes since I have eaten a thing."

"What's got you out this early in the morning?" Donald asked.

"Well, I'll just tell you, Donald. I bought myself a new rifle after my crops came in, and I want to go squirrel hunting today to try it out. I figure this is the best gun I've ever had my hands on, and squirrel season's a wasting. Well, you want to go or not?" Doyle questioned.

"Well, you need to settle down and tell me where you're going, first," Donald replied.

"Well, I have just been pondering about going back in the mountain where Esther lives," Doyle laughed.

"Oh, heck no," Donald shook his head. "You are *not* getting me to go into that mountain where I'll have to cross the bridge where Esther drowned."

Doyle laughed so hard as Donald finished his protest that he spit coffee out all over his shirt. "Don't tell me you believe that old tale," said Doyle. "Of all people, I didn't figure you for a coward."

"You think I'm a coward, do you? Well, I have heard enough from people who have tried to cross that bridge after dark that staying away from there just makes good sense to me," Donald laughed.

"Don, I'm not planning on staying in the woods until dark. I'll be out and home by suppertime," Doyle pleaded.

"Maybe you will, and maybe you won't," said Donald. "I have been in the woods with you many times, and I know how you are when the squir-rels are squawking. You'll stay in the woods as long as you think you can kill one."

"Well, you are going to miss out on a good mess of squirrels," Doyle warned.

"Doyle, you just go on ahead and hit the woods. I think I can manage to kill a mess of squirrel somewhere else," Donald insisted.

So, with his new rifle and squirrel pin in hand, Doyle went on his way to the cool, colorful mountain where according to tradition, Esther waited for a ride across the bridge where she drowned. Doyle never gave Esther another thought; except that he wanted to get across the bridge and out of the woods before dark.

By the time Doyle got to the place on the mountain where he wanted to hunt, squirrels were running everywhere. Doyle killed so many squir-rels that his squirrel pin was loaded down. He never stopped to eat or rest because he loved to hunt, especially since he had a new gun. As a matter of fact, Doyle was so caught up in his hunting adventure that he lost all track of time. This was an unfortunate mistake on Doyle's part. The sun was beginning to set, and shadows were quickly falling over the mountains. Looking around, Doyle suddenly realized that he needed to make his way out of the mountains in a very hasty manner. Having Esther on his back was the only thing he could think of, at his point. Moreover, he prayed that his lingering in the mountains didn't prove Donald right. Only his effort to get across the bridge before dark, and time, would tell.

Before Doyle could make it halfway out of the mountains, the sky was already dusky dark. He quickly realized that it would be dark when he crossed the bridge where Esther, as the story was told, loved to take her ghostly ride. The wooden bridge that spanned the small clear creek lay only about half a mile ahead. This short hike would give Doyle a little time to decide if he was going to cross the ghostly bridge in the dark, or if he would spend the night in woods and risk the dangers of a bear or wildcat. Doyle had to admit that he had gotten himself into one more predicament.

Doyle stopped frantically trying to reach the bridge. Instead, he walked at a steady pace while thinking about what he was going to do. Soon, Doyle's thinking time came to an end. Looking down, Doyle could see the famous bridge just a few yards ahead of him. The young man could feel his flesh tingle; his skin seemed to crawl. He was so scared that losing all control of his senses did not seem far away. Suddenly, Doyle started to laugh. *What am I doing, thinking about some stupid ghost story people tell around their campfire, and acting like a ten-year-old boy? I don't have to stay in these mountains, have my squirrels spoil, and risk my life staying in the deep woods after dark. I'm going home.*

Doyle had talked himself into crossing the bridge, where Esther had fallen into the cold water and drowned, without much effort at all. So, with great pains, Doyle gathered his rifle and held on tight to his squirrel pin. Backing up so he could gather sped before he reached the bridge, Doyle shot out of his tracks running as fast as his legs could carry him. Doyle knew that in just a few seconds he would be across the bridge and headed for home with his bounty of squirrels. He had mustered up his courage, but Esther was still heavy on his mind.

Unfortunately, Doyle had never been so wrong as he was about getting home with his goods. As soon as his foot touched the bridge, he immediately felt Esther jump onto his back and lock her bony arms around his neck. Doyle could feel her sharp knees pressing into his sides. Turning around and around on the bridge, he tried to grab the arms of his bony passenger and pull her off. The ghastly figure refused to release her grip, holding on to Doyle's neck even tighter. In his confusion, Doyle had run the wrong way, and lost both his gun and squirrels on the same side of the bridge that he had started from.

After what seemed an eternity, Doyle finally managed to cross the footbridge, which was only a few feet long. When he made it to the opposite side of the bridge, the skeleton that had been clutching his back disappeared as fast as it had attached itself to his warm body. Weak from his ghostly experience, Doyle found a stump and sat down to get his breath. He could still smell the stench the creature left behind. Suddenly, he realized that he didn't have his new gun, or the squirrels he had worked all day to collect. Looking back, he could see his prized possessions laying on the opposite side of the bridge. Doyle had to decide if he wanted Esther to ride his back again, or if he wanted to leave his gun and squirrels in the mountains. The decision Doyle had to make didn't take long. Rising to his feet, he turned and started from the mountains in a steady run, not stopping until he was safe at home.

Doyle never went back across that bridge again. Moreover, he never recovered his new rifle or his squirrels. Most of all, Doyle never again doubted anything else that Donald told him. He had learned an important lesson where ghosts were concerned. Doyle would never again take a good ghost story lightly the rest of his life. Maybe, just maybe, Doyle was afraid of ghosts after all.

HISTORY LESSON

BEV FREEMAN

History Professor Jan Hornburg took his students to local battlefields to observe re-enactments and write their assessment of life and death in the 1860s. Today's study was in Carter County, at Sycamore Shoals. The portrayal was the Battle of Bull's Gap in Greene County, where a Confederate company tried to overtake a Union stronghold and run them out of East Tennessee. The victory was a temporary one for Major General John Breckinridge.

After the battle, the students mingled with the soldiers and questioned the practicality of their wool uniforms in the autumn heat. Some students inspected the weapons and equipment used by the soldiers.

One small group of students slipped into the underbrush out of sight of their professor to sneak a cigarette. Two girls and three boys sat on a log in front of a spent campfire, passing the hand-rolled smoke between them. One of the girls, Susan, noticed the flicker of warm coals under the scorched sticks. She stirred the embers and added some dead grass, rekindling the fire.

On the stump of an old tree nearby appeared a soldier wearing a tattered uniform in Union colors. Each person in the group looked at the others and back at the soldier. "Where'd you come from?" Tom asked.

The soldier threw up his chin in the direction of the battlefield. "Yonder."

11

"You all got whooped, didn't you?" Victor laughed.

"No, we ain't even begun to fight," said the soldier.

The students all laughed.

"You are Southern sympathizers!" The soldier stood, pointing his rifle at them. "We don't take prisoners. My CO will do away with you."

The group laughed as they passed the smoke again.

"Don't get carried away with this re-enactment mumbo-jumbo, Man." One of the boys said. He stood, stepping toward the Union soldier.

With one swift move, the bayonet at the end of the soldier's rifle thrust into the belly of the young man. He fell to the ground, blood spurting out. The girls screamed. Tom and Victor lunged toward their friend. They discovered the blood was real, and the soldier was gone.

Screams brought other students and Professor Hornburg to the scene.

"What happened here?" Hornburg cried out. "Someone call 911! Get an ambulance here quick!"

More of the students ran to the wooded campsite, and finally soldiers in Confederate uniforms. One threw off his coat and dropped to his knees over the bleeding boy. "I'm a doctor. What happened here?"

He worked to expose the injury, and held the open slit closed with one hand. From his pocket, he pulled a white handkerchief, covering the wound. "Does anyone have a clean shirt or something to plug this wound?"

One of the girls stepped forward and handed her white scarf to the doctor. One of the boys pulled his tube socks off and gave them to the man for a bandage. The doctor tied the scarf around the boy's middle to secure the socks and the handkerchief.

The doctor snapped out orders to the students who were closest. "Two of you grab his arms, a couple more of you get his feet, and I'll get his midsection. We need to get him out of this underbrush and over to that clearing."

Victor and Tom moved to grasp the boy's legs and went with the group. Susan held Bella's arm.

"Wait, let them go." The two girls stood and watched as all the others left the woods.

"Where did he go?" Susan asked.

"He wasn't real," said Bella. "We all imagined this. You know what we were smoking, don't you?"

"No, this is real blood on the ground. The soldier was real, and that bayonet was real. Where is he?"

"Right behind you."

The voice caused the hair to stand up on Bella's neck. She and Susan turned slowly to see blood dripping from that deadly bayonet at the end of a rifle held by an imaginary soldier. "Move," he motioned toward the river.

The girls stepped over logs and downed trees, moving as instructed toward the river. The soldier stayed close behind them. "Where are you taking us?" Susan asked.

"To my CO. Keep walking."

"You do know the war was over a hundred and fifty years ago, right?" Bella asked.

"Stop talking. I know what I'm doing." The soldier nudged Bella with his rifle butt.

"Okay," she said. "We're going. We'll do what you say."

As they approached the river, they saw a small dinghy tied up at the shore. A thick fog hid the opposite bank of the river.

"Get in," he ordered.

The girls stepped in carefully, trying not to tip it over. Then the soldier untied the rope and stepped in behind them. He used a long pole to push off from the bank and into the fog.

The ambulance siren sounded, rushing to the nearby hospital. Professor Hornburg sent Victor and Tom to stay with their friend.

"Where are Susan and Bella? I know they were with these guys. Look for them around that fire, and bring those juvenile delinquents to me," said Hornburg.

"They were there in the woods," one guy spoke up. "But they aren't anywhere around here now."

"Check in the restrooms, Shelby. You fellows look in the vans. They didn't just vanish. They're hiding someplace. I want to know what happened down there!" Hornburg walked toward the re-enactment site.

Shelby checked all the ladies' restrooms and reported back to Hornburg that Susan and Bella weren't there. The two guys said the girls weren't in the vans, either.

Hornburg asked the soldiers to help locate the missing students. They fanned out in a grid pattern, searching from the highway to the river, but came up with no girls.

Two hours later, Tom returned from the hospital. The good news was that their friend, Freddy, was out of surgery and would be okay. Victor had volunteered to stay with him until his parents could drive over from Kingsport.

Hornburg escorted all the students back to the vans, and the drivers took them back to ETSU in Johnson City. Tom chose to remain with the professor, to continue searching for the girls.

They returned to the campsite, where Tom told his instructor the fantastic account of what had happened.

Hornburg laughed and kicked the coals of the campfire. "That must have been some good stuff you were smoking! In the sixties, when I was in college, we didn't get such good quality weed. I want some of that!"

"Freddy brought it. I have no idea where he gets it. But one joint between the five of us was not that misleading. Something happened here. And I'm telling you the sober truth!" Tom swallowed hard, looking at the bloodstain on the ground. "He was young, maybe even younger than me. He looked scared. His eyes were black and cold. As soon as my eyes left him and went to Freddy, he vanished, up in smoke. Seriously!" Tom dropped to his knees, pointing at the ground. "Look; here are his footprints, right below this stump. That's where he stood."

Professor Hornburg knelt down to examine the print in the sand. "Okay, it's not a sneaker print, but it could have been left here last night by one of the soldiers."

"But it rained just as we got here this morning, remember?" Tom said. "This looks like the girls' prints, going off toward the river. And look at this boot print; it's just like that one."

"Okay, let's follow the trail and see if the girls show up," said Professor Hornburg, with a sigh.

The professor and his student walked through the underbrush. At the river's edge, they saw the impression of a small boat or canoe. That's when they noticed the fog.

"That's odd; there's no fog anywhere else around," Professor Hornburg said, observing the strange anomaly. "Didn't we see a canoe up by the fort?"

"Yeah, it's used when they do the Sycamore Shoals Indian battle."

Tom ran in the direction of the fort, followed by his professor.

They returned with the canoe, launched it, and paddled toward the fog. Professor Hornburg took out his phone and snapped a photo of the river where the fog began. He laid the phone on the floor of the canoe and picked up the paddle again. The current was rough, pushing them downriver and deeper into the mist. There was no turning back. The boat took on a mind of its own as the rapids became increasingly aggressive. The mist was so thick the two men couldn't see beyond the end of their paddles. They were not controlling their path; all they could do was hold on.

In a few minutes, they floated out of the rapids and the fog at the same time. The riverbank was about twenty-five feet away, so they steered toward a grassy landing. Tom stepped onto dry land first, followed by the professor. The sky looked exceptionally bright, unlike the clouds they'd seen previously that day.

In the distance, they noticed a small log cabin—but it didn't look old. Tom led the way to the structure through the tall grass. Finding no one around, he knocked on the door. No one came, but the door opened a crack. Tom let himself in.

"Look at this, Professor. It's like we stepped back in time. There's nothing electrical in here. Look at all these cool antiques."

"Wow; this looks authentic, all right. Let's look around outside." The professor stepped back outside, leaving the cabin doorway open. Tom followed closely.

They spotted a small garden with corn, beans, and squash growing together. There were several tomato plants with sticks to climb. They saw potato plants, cabbage, and banana peppers. Beyond the garden stood a shed. When they investigated, they found a corn crib; beyond that was a barn.

"Maybe it's milking time. Let's see if there's someone in the barn." Hornburg said, and led the way. They found a man dressed in old-style clothing and carrying a milk bucket.

"Hello, friends. What brings you all the way out here?" the man asked.

"We're looking for two missing girls, my students from the university. They might be in the company of a man in a uniform."

"No, haven't seen anyone 'round here in weeks, 'cept for you two gents." He set the bucket down, saying, "Where are my manners? I'm

Elijah; this is my homestead." He stuck out a hand to be shaken.

"I'm Jan Hornburg, and this is Tom, another of my students." He shook the man's right hand, noticing its rough texture.

"Howdy, Tom," Elijah shook hands with Tom. "I was just about to eat me some stew. Come to my cabin and join me, will you?"

"Thanks, but no; we need to keep looking for the girls, before it gets any later." The professor asked, "How far is it to your closest neighbor?"

"Miles, I don't even know for sure how many, but it's a day's ride by horse, that way." He pointed north.

"What about Elizabethton? It's just across the river." Tom scratched his head.

"Elizabeth town? I ain't heard of that. You must be mixed up. Did you come by boat?"

"Yes, we did. We've been over at Sycamore Shoals, watching the re-enactment exercise. You know, the old settlement across the river?"

Elijah stepped backward, picking up the bucket. "You gents are a long way from any community or town. I don't know what a re-enactment is, but maybe if you eat something, your mind will clear." He turned and walked toward his cabin.

"What's going on? Did you notice the way he talked, and his clothes? They were nothing like threads we wear. Look around; do you see the houses that are supposed to be high on that hill, overlooking the river? See any electric or telephone wires?" Hornburg felt his pants pocket. "My phone! I must have left it in the canoe. Let's go back to the river."

The two walked back across the grassy field toward the river. There was no fog, no canoe, and worst of all, no phone.

"Maybe it floated downriver. Let's follow the edge and see if we can find our canoe, or the boat the girls crossed on." The professor held an optimistic attitude, but felt confused.

"There should be a bridge in less than a mile. You know, at the boat launch?" Tom asked.

"We'll go a short distance downstream, and then back up. We know there's a bridge close to where the Doe River joins the Watauga." He tested his student's mood: "If we're still in our century, that is."

Tom forced a chuckle, but didn't look as if he felt amused.

The two had walked about a quarter mile before they discovered a small skiff wedged into the bushes on the river's edge. They headed inland to see if the girls left a trail. And yes, there was a ribbon from Bella's braid, hanging in a blueberry bush. They continued walking. Soon, a patch of sand revealed one large boot print and two small ladies' sneaker prints.

Tom dropped to his knees and motioned for the professor to get down. "Did you hear that?"

"Sounded like horses."

"Right. We need to stay quiet." Tom led the way. As a hunter, he knew the importance of a stealthy approach.

In a clearing ahead, they saw horses tied on a rope line stretched between two trees. Several tents were set up in a group next to a large campfire. They saw one man sitting next to a smaller fire, with iron pots over the blaze. Beyond the clearing, they heard laughter and loud taunting voices. Slipping closer, behind the horses, they were in sight of a group of rough looking men surrounding the two girls.

"There they are," Tom whispered.

The professor nodded and looked back at the animals. "If we release and scatter the horses, maybe the men will chase them and we can grab the girls."

"That's what John Wayne would do," Tom laughed. He worked his way around to the rope securing the horses, untied it, and slid all their reins off the rope. Then he jumped up, raising his arms high and flapping them, alarming the skittish animals.

The men quickly turned their attention to the noise of the horses stampeding away. They ran after them, just as the professor hoped. Tom whistled, and the girls ran toward him. A lone soldier chased them. Bella tripped, falling face down to the ground. The soldier grabbed her, jerking the girl to her feet. Tom tackled the soldier, and Bella ran to the professor. Tom easily overtook the slightly built boy, knocking him out with one blow to his face.

The professor had sent both girls running toward the river. Tom caught up and helped Bella, who kept stumbling. Susan reached the skiff first and pushed it into the river. She and the professor had boarded by the time Tom and Bella arrived.

"We can't all four get in. I'll stay hidden in the bushes, and you get the girls out of here," Tom said.

"No, get in; we'll make it work. We all need to stick together. I'm still not sure what's happening here," the professor said.

Tom squeezed in, sitting behind Bella. The professor clenched the long pole and pushed them into the current. As they floated away, the soldiers reached the edge of the river. Some fired their muskets, and others waded into the river to give chase.

The rapids grew strong, pushing the skiff with its heavy load between the rocks and into deep water. The pole could no longer reach the bottom to propel the craft. The wind blew strong out of the west, sending the four runaways into the fog.

After a few minutes of rough waters and threatening rain, the sky cleared and the skiff came to a bridge. Professor Hornburg poled to the river's edge and climbed out on the shore opposite of where they had loaded up.

"Let me take a look around. You three stay out of sight. Hide under the bridge 'til I get back," the professor directed. Hornburg scurried up the bank to the road as Susan poled them into the shade of the bridge. Tom noticed the support underneath was iron, and from a more recent decade than the soldiers.

After about fifteen minutes, Hornburg returned. The look on his face was not encouraging. He sat on the side of the riverbank. "How can this be possible? The road is asphalt, but no cars are traveling on it, and it looks like it might have bomb holes in places. I should have seen some sign of civilization, but there's nothing there."

The three students looked at each other. Then Susan spoke up. "One of the soldiers was talking about the president's assassination. I got the idea he meant Abe Lincoln. I think it's the fog causing a time warp. Maybe if we walk back upriver on this side, through the mist, we'll get back to our era."

"Do you know how crazy that sounds?" Bella cried.

"Yes, we do, but how else can you explain what happened to Freddy, you two, and now all four of us? We've experienced two, possibly three, periods in history. If we can retrace our steps, it might work." Hornburg stood up. "Come on, let's hide the skiff further up under the bridge, just in case we need to make a run for it again."

The fog felt cold against their faces as they walked, hand in hand.

The professor led the way, and Tom brought up the rear. Just a few yards into the depths, they began hearing sounds all around and catching an occasional glimpse of people passing close by them. They heard sounds of aircraft overhead, and explosions in the distance. Was this attack on their future world?

At one point Susan paused, letting go of the professor's hand. She screamed as if something happened to injure her. Hornburg grabbed her bloody hand, pulling her toward him.

"Don't look at the sides. Keep holding hands, moving forward. Don't stop, no matter what!"

In seconds, the blood disappeared from Susan's hand. She held tightly to Bella and the professor. A blizzard whipped through, chilling them for a moment, and then it was gone. Hornburg walked around an enormous boulder, making sure his students stayed close. On the other side, they felt the heat of a raging fire. Breathing became difficult, and it was hard to see their path. As quickly as it appeared, the blaze was gone, and a soft rain fell. Voices of people out of sight came next; it sounded as if someone was crying. More than one wail of grief reached them, maybe from a crowd of mourners, then they passed a long line of fresh graves—but there were no markers. Continuing, they met shadows of people, transparent and drifting through them like the fog itself. One floated into Tom's face and screamed. He used his free hand to wipe it away. Another came at Bella.

"Don't let go; they're trying to separate us!" Tom yelled over the wind whirling around them. He squeezed Bella's hand tighter.

The wind stopped suddenly. The sun came out, and the fog was gone in an instant. They stood on the riverbank, in the spot where their experience had begun. They continued holding hands as they walked through the woods, back toward the re-enactment grounds and the old fort.

They heard gunfire, and saw smoke rising from little explosions. Freddy came running toward them, followed by Victor.

"Where have you guys been? You missed the best battle ever!" He slapped his professor on the shoulder.

"Are you feeling okay, Freddy?" Tom asked.

"Sure, and I have a whole new appreciation for history now, Professor Hornburg. I promise I won't slack on my assignments again. Watching history in progress holds my attention."

"Well, that's nice, Freddy. And I can assure you, we haven't missed any part of the history lesson today. Right, girls?"

Tom, Bella, and Susan laughed, but never revealed the joke. They knew today was an experience they'd never forget, and also hoped never to revisit.

Obed's Curse

Sharyn Martin

Rain spattering against the dirty window caused little gray rivers, distorting the view of the backyard and smokehouse. Maude Darnell wiped the window with her sleeve, but it just made a bigger smudge. Turning to the wooden table, she took a biscuit from the pan and crumbled it into a chipped bowl, added a spoonful of pale, congealed gravy, and mixed it as she walked to the door. Pulling her old coat over her head, she stepped off the porch into the rain, moving carefully across the flat rock walkway to the smokehouse. Taking a wad of keys from her pocket, she unlocked the large padlock on the hasp, carefully opened the door, and peered into the darkness.

"Here. You've got to eat. I won't let you starve."

What appeared to be a pile of rags shifted in the corner and sat up. Squinting at the small bit of light coming through the door, the man came to life. He moved slowly, crawling across the dirt floor, dragging one leg. His swollen ankle would not allow him to stand, and the chain on his other leg was anchored to the wall on a big rusty bolt. The cut above his right eye was crusting over. Maude set the bowl on the floor and moved back to the door. The man reached toward the bowl and pulled it toward him. He used his grimy fingers to scrape the food into his mouth and licked the sides of the bowl.

"I'll bring you some water in a little while. Can't have you dying yet."

"God, Woman. How long are you going to keep me here? I've been here for days. Nobody knows if I'm dead or alive."

"Far as I know, nobody cares," said Maude.

"Why are you doing this? What'd I ever do to you, you crazy old woman?"

Maude backed out the door, shutting it tight, and fastened the lock. Across the road, the Holston River was rising. It had been raining solidly for three days and nights. The sky didn't appear to be lightening up, and Maude figured the rain would keep on. Didn't matter to her, one way or the other. She'd lived here for over fifty years in the same shack, and she guessed she'd die here. Only once in all the years had the river got up to the porch.

Maude's captive lay back down on the floor. The stench in the small, dark building was almost unbearable. His toilet was a small area behind the old plow. His chain would only reach so far, and his broken ankle wouldn't allow any more movement. Lying on the floor with his eyes closed, he tried to think. *Why am I here? I never bothered this woman. Who is she? Does anybody know I'm missing? Lord, I know I haven't lived a decent life, but please don't let me die here.*

Maude opened the front door, walked out on the porch, and looked toward the road. The water was coming up toward the house. The road was several yards away from her house in the hollow, and the river just beyond the road. This meant the water was rising faster than the day before. A willow tree was slumping across the inlet of water. The soggy soil wasn't going to hold it much longer. She shut the door and went back to the table and sat there, looking toward the smokehouse, straining to see through the filthy window. Cracked and dirty dishes cluttered the table and a big, black bug skittered across the edge.

Obed McClain had been on her mind for the last few days, stronger than before. She thought back to the time when they were something special—or at least, *she* thought they were. People around the hollow used to say what a pretty couple they were. He was the most handsome man she'd ever seen, and she'd given him all she had. He laughed when she told him she was going to have his child, and said, "Did you think I was going to marry you?" He was going to Roanoke, where he'd get a job, and maybe find a woman up there. He left the week after she told him about the child, and Maude swore from that day on that she would curse his life and his children's lives. She was glad her parents were dead; it was the first time she'd ever felt that way.

Maude had gone over to Sawyer Creek and found the midwife. The potion the woman had given her worked, and Maude came back home empty. There was no baby, and no one ever knew why Obed had left. The old homeplace had burned while Maude was in Sawyer Creek, leaving her with no more than what she had taken with her. The Jones place had been empty for some time, so Maude took over the shack near the river. The years wore on, and Maude was considered an outcast by what few neighbors she had. Children ran by the house, yelling "witch woman" when they had cleared the yard. Maude would set on the porch, watching the river and cursing the youngsters as they fled.

She heard a crash and looked out. The willow had pulled from the bank and was lying partially submerged in the small inlet to the house. The rain was coming down harder. Maude opened the door further and went out on the porch. The water was coming faster and faster. She sat on the cane bottomed chair she'd brought from the kitchen and watched the willow leaves, waving like green hair in the swift water.

Rase thought back to last week. He had come to the mountain to hunt for game. He remembered his daddy telling him what a fine place this was for rabbit, deer, and squirrel. Rase had only been here once before, to find the cabin that had belonged to his daddy, and to his granddaddy before that. He figured it would make a good hunting refuge. He didn't realize the cliff was so close when he was walking across the side of the hill. The last thing he remembered was sliding down the hill. He woke up in a smelly building with an old woman looking down at him.

Maude had dragged the young man from the briars and bushes to the smokehouse after hearing something groaning just out from the garden. She knew who he was as soon as she saw him, and she figured God had sent him to her.

The water came closer, washing against the porch. Maude just waited, watching the animals and tree limbs float by. *A few more hours and it'll start to go down*, she thought. It would have to crest sometime.

The afternoon brought heavier rain pounding against the windows, the river coming up to the floor of the house. Maude had to get off the porch; she went to the back of the house. The water was beginning to come under the door. She lay down on the cot by the back door, pulling the ragged curtain over the window. *It will be better in the morning*, she thought and closed her eyes.

Rase awoke during the night, his ankle throbbing in pain. He heard the rain hammering the roof, and felt the water around him. He tried to get up, but the chain jerked him back and his ankle gave way. Pulling against the chain, he finally gave up in exhaustion. The water was over his feet now. As he lay there thinking about his life and what he would miss most, the door to the smokehouse twisted away from the frame. He felt the rush of water coming over his legs, and he was lifted and pushed against the wall.

The chain snapped under the water's assault, and he was washed through the door. The slope of the mountain behind the smokehouse loomed over him. Small trees struggled to stay rooted to the bank. Grabbing one of the maple saplings, Rase pulled himself up the slope. He cried out as he scraped his legs against the sharp rocks. He could look down on what was left of the house and the horrible smokehouse that had been his home the past few days. Maude was nowhere to be seen.

John Reed and his son, Anderson, came from across the river in their small boat to survey the damage and what was left of Maude's shack. The stone steps to the porch were still in place, and the foundation was still there. The house was gone; the only evidence of the smokehouse was a chimney, left standing by the flood for some reason. John heard a sound coming from the hill. Looking up, he saw a man clinging to a small tree, looking more dead than alive. John and Anderson waded through the water inside the foundation of Maude's house, pulling the boat beside them. They eased the man down the slope and into the boat.

Anderson pulled off his coat and put it over the man's shoulders. The small boat was slapping against the rocks jutting from the hillside.

"Who are you, Son?" John Reed asked.

"My name is Rase McClain," the man muttered.

"Not from around here, are you?"

"No Sir, I'm from just outside Roanoke. I just came down here to hunt, and had a bad fall. I nearly broke my ankle and I hit my head when I fell, and I woke up in this God-forsaken barn—and some crazy old woman kept calling me 'Obed.' She kept talking about a dead baby. I'm just glad to be away from her. Who is she?"

"Her name is Maude Darnell. Nobody bothers her much. She's lived here on this riverbank for over fifty years."

"Well, 'Obed' was my granddaddy's name. Guess she must have known him, or had me mixed up with somebody else."

The Reeds pushed the boat around what was left of Maude's place. Nobody noticed the gray hair swirling among the willow leaves.

ONLY TIME WILL TELL

LINDA HUDSON HOAGLAND

The old neighborhood was nearly unrecognizable. I wasn't sure if the neighborhood had changed as much as I thought it had, or if the vision that was permanently planted in my brain was that far off.

I climbed from my car and strolled the same old cracked sidewalk I'd wandered over when I was younger, and new to the world of being a city dweller.

I didn't know if I should go up to the front door of the house where I used to live and knock for admittance into a room of memories. The people living there were complete strangers, but the house was an old friend.

"Hi, my name is Ellen. You don't know me, but I used to live in this house, several years ago," I explained hurriedly as I smiled broadly.

"What do you want?" the unshaven, barely dressed man asked brusquely.

"Could I take a peek inside? I was trying to remember how it was laid out, because I'm writing a short story about my life here. I moved away a long time ago, but I still have some strong memories of living here," I explained hurriedly, watching his face cloud up a bit from what I thought was anger.

"Do you have any idea of what goes on in this house?" he asked in a harsh voice.

"What do you mean?" I asked, trying to look innocent.

26

"The noises! The voices, the banging, the strange people walking, or maybe I should say floating, up and down the stairs to the second floor!" he sputtered.

"I'm sorry," I said, trying not to smile. "I don't know what you mean."

"This place is haunted. You lived here. You know it's haunted!" he screamed at me.

"Tell me, what is happening? What makes you think it's haunted?" I asked. I tried to suppress my all-knowing smile.

"It doesn't happen all the time, but I never know when it's going to happen," he said. He started his tale of woe, slightly calmer.

"What happens?" I probed.

"The ghosts, they come out during the night on their schedule, and I haven't figured out when that is. I never know when they're going to keep me up all night. It happened last night. I don't know why, but they started up at about midnight, and kept that racket up until three this morning. They seemed to be celebrating something. They weren't out to do me any harm, not last night. They just kept me awake with their noise," he said with a sigh.

"You said they didn't do you any harm last night; have they caused you harm previously?" I asked.

"Yes, they have," he answered.

"Will you tell me about it?" I asked.

"No... I don't think so," he answered, looking down at the floor.

"Have you done any research on the house?" I asked.

"Where would I go to do that?" he asked angrily.

"I went to the courthouse to see who owned the house years ago, then I went to the newspaper office to find some old articles about the goings on here. They used to keep me awake a lot. I'm sorry you are having the same problem," I said as I tried to show sympathy.

"You said you didn't know what I meant, but you do. What did you do to make them stop?" he asked, raking his fingers through his hair while keeping his eyes closed.

"I didn't. I couldn't. They wouldn't go away when I lived here. My only answer was to move away from here," I explained.

"I can't afford to move. I just lost my job for being late to work too many times. Can you guess why?" he snarled.

"How much would it cost to get you moved?" I asked, with all of the sympathy I could muster.

"Why would you do that?" he asked in astonishment flavored with skepticism.

"I know what you are going through. Believe me, I do," I said reassuringly.

"What do you want, Lady?" the man demanded. "Really? No one would offer to give me money to move, especially since I'm unemployed," he said flatly.

"I don't want anything. I just want to help. That's all, I promise you," I answered.

I really did have an ulterior motive for my kind action of helping the man. I wanted to move back into the house and do some more investigating on my own. The house was drawing me back into its dark, splintery, wooden arms, and I couldn't fight it anymore.

"You haven't told me your name," I said to the burly, unshaven man.

"It's Titus Moore, and it would cost about a thousand bucks to get me out of here. I would gladly move if you would give me the money," he said with a half-smile. His lips were smiling but his eyes hadn't received the message.

"May I look around?" I asked sweetly.

"Go ahead, Lady," he said as he walked away to answer the ringing telephone.

I walked upstairs and saw that he did not use the rooms up there for anything except storage. Everything was the same as it was when I left, other than the boxes piled the middle of each bedroom, of which there were two plus an unfinished attic area.

The house was old; the plaster was crumbling and the floors were sagging, but I wanted to move back in and start anew in the house where I had spent a good deal of my life.

"When do you want the money to move?" I asked when I re-entered the living room

"I've been checking on a place down the street. If you would walk down there with me, you can give the man the deposit and the first and last months' rent. That will come to eight hundred dollars, and I can use the other two hundred dollars to get everything transferred from here to the new place in my name. Would you really do that?" he asked skeptically.

"Sure. Let's go now," I suggested, reaching for my checkbook.

It was about three houses away and the required payment was eight hundred dollars, just as he told me. That meant that he had been planning to move as soon as he could scrape the money together.

"When do you think you can get your things out?" I asked.

"I'll be out of here today. The house came furnished, so I don't have a lot to move."

"That's good," I said, with a broad smile.

"Why are you so interested in getting me out of here? I want the truth this time," he demanded.

"I want to move back into this house and find out why all of the scary stuff happens." I explained.

"Who owns this house? I pay the rent to a real estate company. He didn't tell me who it belongs to. He wouldn't do anything about the haunting. He accused me of making it up," Titus said angrily.

"The house belonged to my Aunt Bessie, but she died. That's why the real estate company was the one to collect the rent. She left it to me, and I want to live in it," I said.

"Lady, you can move in with my blessings, but don't say that I didn't warn you," he said. He grabbed the check for $200 from my hand, the balance of the thousand dollars I'd offered.

Titus did just as he said he would. He was out and gone, with all utilities paid and out of his name, by the next day. He really *did* want out.

I moved in after I cleaned up and tossed out items I no longer wanted.

The first night I slept in the house, I had no visitors.

I was so disappointed.

I really wanted to see my cousin Stella, along with her kids, Buzzy and Betsy. They were some of the people Titus heard, and they meant no harm.

The next night, I was sitting on the bed looking around, taking in all of the atmosphere of a haunted house.

"Stella, how are you doing?" I asked the air.

Of course, there was no response.

I was talking to a ghost.

The curtain moved a bit, so I knew she was with me.

"Is he here?" I asked, rapidly scanning the room. There was a heavy, dangerous feeling in the air.

The door suddenly opened and slammed closed.

The room seemed to sigh, as if it were letting out a held breath. The room was lighter and happier.

"Stella, he's mad at me because I'm back. He will go away and not bother you now. You and the kids can go on living here in peace, if that's what you want," I said. I smiled and stretched out on the bed.

Lloyd, the unfriendly ghost, wasn't going to stay around me. He knew that I knew his secret; I knew that he did it. He killed them all in a drunken rage.

With Lloyd out of the house, maybe Stella and the kids would go to the great beyond. I was planning to stay and watch to see if that happened.

Hopefully, Lloyd wouldn't feel the need to return to the house to kill me, if Stella and the kids leave.

Only time will tell.

So They Say...

Willie E. Dalton

They say black panthers don't live in this part of the country. But the people who say that don't live around here. Ask any of the older people who live back in the hollers: They'll tell you stories about hearing them at night, roaming hungry and fierce through the mountains, screaming like a woman being killed. The older folks laugh when people say "they don't live here," because they know better.

My daddy always kept us kids close to the house when it started getting dark. Other kids would be out running around the woods until they couldn't see their hand in front of their face. Daddy would let us play in the yard until near bedtime. But he wanted us home, where he could watch us from his rocker on the porch with his .22 beside him, leaned against the house. I didn't really know why, but I knew better than to disobey him.

After a ten-hour workday in the mines, Daddy would come home and work in the garden. One night, when I was about twelve, Daddy and I went out on the porch. His jeans and shirt were dirty from working in the garden, and his red cap sat somewhat askew on his sweating head. Moths flitted around the light above the screen door, and the sound of the frogs out in the darkness was a loud, steady background noise. Daddy slowly rocked back and forth in his worn old chair. He had a wad of tobacco in his jaw, and stared out into the yard as the last bit of light faded.

I sat down on the floor of the porch beside him and looked up at him.

31

"Daddy, why do you get nervous when it gets dark out?" I asked him, wondering if he'd tell me.

He glanced down at me for a moment, eyes trying to discern if he should tell me or not. Then he stared back out at the yard. He spit in the can he kept on the porch (Momma wouldn't let him chew in the house) and cleared his throat.

"I wasn't too much older than you when my daddy and your uncle was makin' and sellin' moonshine. People got caught and arrested for it all the time. If they didn't get caught makin' it, they got caught carryin' it. My brother had the idea to make me carry it across the mountain. It wouldn't be likely for anyone to stop a kid. If someone did stop me, I was just supposed to say I was on my way to Papaw's house, or make up something. Daddy wasn't sure about the idea, but his friends in the next town said they'd help look out for me, so he agreed. Every Friday night after school, I'd come home and load up my bag with jars of 'shine and start walking. It would take me a couple of hours to get to the meeting spot. 'Shine delivered and money in my pocket, I'd start walkin' home. I did it for a couple of years, and Daddy paid me a little to do it, so I didn't mind."

He stopped talking and adjusted his hat, just to give his hands something to do. He sighed and spit in the can again before continuing his story.

"I was walkin' back, it was probably about eleven o'clock at night. There was a big full moon out; it was just huge, and yellow, and lit up the path. I'd always heard the tale of weird things being out on full moons, so I was always a little more watchful. But the closer I got to the house, the more relaxed I got. I had my empty bag slung over my shoulder and was shufflin' my feet along, hummin' some tune or another, when I heard a sound that chilled me to the bone. I swear to God I thought somebody was being murdered, not fifty feet from me. It was a painful, hair-raising sound. I didn't know what to do. If a body really was hurt, what could I do? I figured I'd just end up getting myself hurt, too—but I couldn't just leave and not even try to help. I hollered, "Is anybody there? Do you need help?" Nobody answered. By that time my stomach was one big knot. The hair on the back of my neck was standin' straight up. All I wanted was to just get home. I started walkin' again, just a whole lot faster. When I got to the house and stepped into the yard, I had a strong urge to turn around. Up

32

on the hill I'd just walked down, sitting pretty as you please, was a wampus cat. Black as pitch, she was; if the moon hadn't been so bright I'd never have seen her. Guess she'd been followin' me the whole way home, trying to decide whether or not I was a good dinner. I told Daddy about it the next day, and he never made me go on another run again."

Daddy's story had been scary up to the point he said wampus cat, and I chuckled. I knew it was what most of the people around here called a panther, but the name was just so silly. It seemed strange for my dad to still be scared of something that happened that long ago. I took my own hat off and ran my fingers through my sweaty hair. I hadn't been home from baseball practice long, and hadn't even changed out of my uniform yet.

"Dad, you've had run-ins with bears and rattlers and plenty of other things that could have killed you. Why did the panther get to ya so much?" I looked at him, puzzled.

He let out a long breath, and I could tell he wanted to reach for the little flask he kept in his pocket, but he didn't. He always tried not to drink in front of the kids.

"Well, I guess it's 'cause your grandpa had an experience with one when he was a young man, too. He and his brothers and sisters were in their room one night. It was a little bitty house, and back then all the kids slept in one room. It was winter, so the more of them that could pile together the warmer they'd be. Anyway, on this night, a noise woke them up. They were used to animal sounds, but this was different. Not too many critters would be out in the snow, and definitely not making that much noise. Strangest of all, it was walking on the roof. They all huddled up together and listened as whatever this thing was walked above their heads. Each step in the frozen snow crunched loudly against the tin roof. They figured it was some kind of monster, and thought at any minute it was going to come crashing through the ceiling and eat them. Finally, it left, and the next morning they went outside and looked up at the roof. They saw huge cat's paw prints across the top of their house where the creature had walked. There was more tracks down on the ground, leading into the woods. Wasn't but a few days after that some people's dogs and small livestock started disappearin'. Grandpa said his daddy had a panther story too, but I don't recall him ever tellin' me." He stopped to spit. "Just seems a bit strange to me that the men in this family have all had encounters with an animal most people 'round here have only heard of. Feels like they're followin' us, or somethin'." He chuckled "I know that sounds silly."

I understood a little more of why Dad was so wary now. "Do you think I'll ever run into one?"

"I hope you never do, Son."

Years passed, and I never forgot the stories Dad told. I never let his stories keep me out of the woods, but I did try to get myself home before dark most nights.

My dad's land was mine now, but I wanted my own house. I built my house just a little farther up the mountain. I didn't clear many trees when I was building; I wanted to be able to look straight into the woods. It was a pretty place, and I still miss it sometimes.

I lived there several years before anything strange happened. One night, I heard something on the deck. I figured it was just a raccoon or possum scrounging around. I flipped on the porch light and didn't see anything, so I didn't think much more about it. That night I went to bed and dreamed there was an old woman in my room. She had long, white hair, and her face was soft and kind. She was wearing a long white nightgown and she smiled gently at me. But as her smile kept growing bigger, I saw there were no teeth. Then, I realized she had no gums, just blackness in a pale white face. She began walking towards me. Her face started to change as she moved closer. The soft lines on her aging face turned hard, deep and menacing. Her long, silky white hair turned yellow and stringy. I watched her crystal blue eyes bleed to black as she approached the side of my bed. As she reached out her bony hand, I saw her fingernails weren't human. Her nails were thick, dark brown, and claw-like. She pinned my arm down.

My heart raced, and I couldn't tell if I was dreaming or awake. I tried to push her arm off of mine, but she wasn't weak as a frail old lady should be. She had the strength of several men. She leaned her upper body over mine, still smiling so I that I saw nothing but blackness. The blackness poured out of her mouth and took the shape of black beetles that ran across me and down under my sheets.

Surrendering to the terror, I screamed. I knew no one could hear me, and I knew no one could rescue me. I screamed because it was all I had left. Then someone screamed back. Someone was screaming louder than me, fiercer than me. It was a sound of pain, anguish, and anger. I didn't even realize I had closed my eyes until they opened. I saw it wasn't the old woman screaming. It was someone or something outside. It was the scream of a panther.

The old woman backed away from me, frantically trying to cover her ears. She backed herself against the wall of my room. Suddenly, she was just gone. The scream outside ended just as quickly. I didn't know if I should I be relieved or more scared.

Sometime later, the adrenaline subsided and sleep took over. The next day, I was left to wonder if everything I had gone through had really happened. I'd never doubted my sanity, but I'd also never seen someone come out of my wall.

I'm not ashamed to admit I wasn't looking forward to going home the next day. I made work drag on longer than usual. I also decided to stop by my buddy's garage before heading home. The fluorescent lights in the garage were harsh as I walked in, and Lynyrd Skynyrd was playing loudly.

"Hey, Sam," I called.

Sam didn't look up from underneath the hood of his truck, but he threw his hand up and waved.

"Get yourself a beer!" He yelled over the music.

I went over to the fridge and did just that. Sam joined me a minute later. He looked me over and wrinkled his eyebrows.

"You look like hell."

I sighed and took off my hat, working the bill over in my hands like my dad used to do. I told Sam about hearing the panther the previous night. I left out the part about the old hag; I just didn't feel like hearing myself say those words out loud.

Sam nodded, "Yeah, every now and then you hear 'em, or hear about 'em." He sipped his beer. "You know we ain't even supposed to have those things around here. They're supposedly not native. My grandad always said there was a legend that if a woman's husband died in a tragic way, that's what she'd become: a panther. That's why they sound like a woman in pain, because she has a broken heart."

"Hmm," was all I could think to say. We talked about cars for a while and finished our beers. Eventually, I decided it was time to head on home. It was nearly dark, and I was starting to think maybe I shouldn't have killed quite so much time.

My driveway was long and narrow, winding up about half a mile through the woods. It was a nightly occurrence to see deer and turkey as I drove. My headlights shone on something laying across the road up ahead. I knew what it was before I got close: another downed tree. "Damn," I swore.

I left the truck running and got out to see if I could move the dead wood. Sometimes big branches were deceiving. They looked heavy, but were light and easy to move after being eaten away by years of rot and decay. Other times, the tree had fallen because it was too heavy for the roots to support it. Those were a beast to move. After a few of those, I'd just started keeping a chainsaw in the truck.

It was too dark to tell much about the tree that had fallen. I tried to push it with my boot, but it didn't budge. I went back to the truck for the chainsaw. I looked the saw over the best I could by the light of my headlights and started it. I breathed a sigh of relief when it started on the first try. I got the first piece of the tree cut and out of the way within just a few minutes. I was almost through the second when the saw started making an odd noise and came to a stop. Something had thrown the chain off track. I could fix it, but not in the dark. It would have to wait until tomorrow. If I wanted to get home, I was walking.

I'd walked my driveway more times than I could count. I had walked it in the daylight and a few times after dark. I never really minded walking the driveway. Nothing bad had ever happened when I had. It was a long, uphill walk. I would arrive home sweaty and out of breath, that's all. But after last night's events, I wasn't looking forward to walking it tonight.

I told myself I was being silly, and to just think about something else until I got home. I turned off my truck lights, grabbed my flashlight and pistol from the glove box, and started walking.

My footsteps crunched loudly in the dirt and gravel as I walked. A screech owl lived up to its name and I nearly jumped out of my skin. I had a bit of a laugh at my own expense as my heart rate slowed back down. The flashlight covered a lot of ground in front of me, but the darkness at my back seemed to follow me, threatening to swallow me up. I walked faster.

The faster I walked, the faster the darkness followed. Soon I was nearly running. Something between a laugh and screech rang through darkness ahead of me and I froze. I wondered if it was another screech owl, making

36

his nightly calls. But I admitted there was something slightly human in the sound. I knew it wasn't an owl. The advancing darkness stopped when I stopped. It hung just at my back as I shined my light in front of me, trying to see where the sound had come from.

I was terrified to look into the darkness and see the old hag coming for me. If I ran, she could chase me. Maybe whatever was following me had gotten ahead of me. I could run into the clutches or claws of whatever had been behind me. I was trapped: paralyzed by fear, with no good options.

I wrapped my hand around my pistol, but it gave me no comfort since I couldn't see whatever was toying with me. My house wasn't much farther ahead. I decided I would have to try to get there. With a deep breath, I took a step. My feet were as heavy as if I were dragging them through wet cement. I concentrated on walking the best I could, one foot in front of the other.

The darkness followed me again as I walked. A hot breeze across the back of my neck made my hair stand up. Another hot puff of air on the back of my neck, and I knew it was not a breeze at all. It was the breath of the thing following behind me. I swallowed hard, but didn't turn around. I just kept moving forward. A deep, guttural growl trickled from the blackness over my shoulder. I knew my end was near. I kept walking, waiting for the panther to take me down. I could see my porch light by then, but it was still at least fifty feet away. I was going to die just outside my own house.

Then, an eerily familiar laugh came. There was no humor in it, only a sickening sense of malice. With another laugh, the hag came out from under the shadows of my deck. The first things I saw were her eyes, pools of emptiness in a pale, withered face. Her stringy hair seemed to whisper in the breeze, and her black dress blended into the shadows so well that it appeared she was only a floating head and hands. Oh, those hands: so pale they were, nearly gray. Her nails looked worse than I remembered, those yellow, jagged claws. She had been waiting for me. Even if I'd driven up in my truck, she could have taken me.

Before she could even begin to move toward me I felt a rush from behind. I braced for the impact and closed my eyes. If one of these things was going to kill me, I'd rather it be the panther—but the beast didn't lunge for me. In one long, graceful movement, the cat sailed past me and landed within inches of the hag. She growled at the hag, then let out one of her screams. It was so loud and piercing, my ears were left ringing. With a leap, the panther grabbed the hag by the throat and started dragging her into the woods. The panther had saved me.

I've played the night over in my head more times than I can count through the years. I don't know where the hag came from, or why she was after me. I've got a hunch about why the panther saved me. There's no family left around here to ask about it, though. When I was little, Daddy told me one of my great-grandfathers was murdered. He left behind a wife and three little kids. The wife was so distraught she went missing only a few weeks later, leaving her sister to raise the kids. Everyone thought she'd drowned herself in the lake. When I remembered Sam's story about the old legend, it made a little sense. Maybe the panther that had followed all the men of my family was related to us. Maybe she was our protector.

I don't live in the woods anymore. I moved a little closer to work. When the subject of panthers comes up, I still hear people declare, "We don't have those around here." I just nod and wink, then respond, "Well, so they say."

THE FOLLOWERS

LINDA HUDSON HOAGLAND

E dwin spotted them the moment he stepped off of the train. They tried to duck behind the partition displaying the posted signs for local businesses, but he saw them clearly before they disappeared from sight.

Edwin knew they would be there, waiting.

They weren't there to greet him, help him carry his luggage, or give him a welcoming hug. They were there to watch him, to scrutinize his every move.

Edwin had thought he'd been gone long enough for them to forget about him. At least, that was his hope.

He walked slowly through the train station. Slow was his only speed, now; age had done that to him. He walked slowly, he talked slowly, and he lived his life slowly. The hurry was gone, as well as the need to hurry. His only goal nowadays was living to the end of each day, hoping to see the sunrise of another day ahead of him.

"Why don't you leave me alone?" he shouted at the group of three that had followed him to the street. "Just leave me alone."

He knew the words were lost amid the traffic sounds. Those to whom he had directed his harangue had all scattered like ants, ducking into this store front or that alley. Once again, he looked like the foolish old man that he was, talking to himself and exhibiting obvious signs of being crazy—or at the very least, senile or suffering from Alzheimer's.

"I'm not crazy," he muttered at the people passing him, arching away from him as if he were carrying some kind of contagion.

Edwin shook his head from side to side while mumbling and walking. He was headed for the motel, where he would rent a room for a day or two until he could get his house opened up and ready for habitation.

The house had been empty for a long time, with only the neighbor looking after it to make sure no vandals got at it to wreak havoc on the only substantial thing he had left in his life.

His arms were tired from carrying the two suitcases. No one bothered to offer him a helping hand, and his followers merely continued to follow him.

"I need a room for a couple of nights, maybe more. I'm just not sure," he explained to the clerk behind the desk, who peered at him suspiciously over the reading glasses perched on his long, straight nose.

"I need a credit card, Sir," the clerk said snidely.

"I'm paying cash," said Edwin.

"I still need a credit card, Sir," insisted the clerk.

"Whatever for? I said I'm paying cash," sputtered Edwin.

"Just as a precaution, sir. We need the card information to use in case you cause any damage to the room."

"Well, I don't have a credit card. I'm Edwin Banks, and I will be living in that big empty house on Walker Lane. There, you will know where to find me if you think I owe you for any damages. I'm going to stay here only until I can get the house opened up and livable."

"I guess we can make an exception to the rule, Mr. Banks, especially since you are local."

"Good. Now, tell me what room," Edwin said, as politely as he could muster.

"Second floor, room 208. The elevator is right over there," the clerk said, pointing to a set of double doors on the other side of the lobby.

Edwin took the key card from the counter and grabbed his two suitcases. Obviously, he wasn't going to get any help, again.

When he entered the elevator, he saw them again. The followers were entering the motel just as the elevator doors closed.

"Oh, God, there they are again," he muttered.

When he reached the second floor, he exited the elevator, trying to make his slow-moving legs step a little faster. He wanted to get into his room before the followers saw which room he had entered.

"Damn," he muttered. "My room is all the way at the end. I hope I can get inside before they get up here."

He dropped his suitcases to the floor and fumbled with the key card.

"I hope this thing works," he whispered as he shoved the key card into the slot and waited for the color of the light to change from red to green.

He grabbed the key card from the slot and turned the handle.

It didn't open.

Again, he shoved the key card into the slot, and he stood poised and ready to open the door immediately, without removing the card.

It worked this time. He reached for one of his suitcases as he held the door open with the other hand. He placed it inside the door and turned to retrieve the second suitcase.

He heard the elevator moving up the shaft. He jerked the second suitcase inside his room before the elevator doors opened.

Edwin walked into his bathroom and placed his ear against the wall. If the followers were in that elevator, they would probably stay in the room next to him.

He stood perfectly still and listened anxiously; the only noise in the room was the sound of his breathing. He held his breath and listened intently.

Nothing. No sounds came to him. Maybe they weren't on that elevator. Maybe they were going to leave him be.

While he'd been gone from this small town, the followers didn't bother him. Those years locked away in prison for vehicular homicide were hard to live through, but the followers never showed up once. They never signed in as visitors trying to see him, and he wasn't harassed by their ever-constant presence.

Now that he had returned home, they met him at the train station and the harassment had started once more.

He grabbed a piece of paper and started writing down their descriptions one by one.

Mary, he decided to call her, was always the first one he saw of the group. Her long blonde hair was dirty and looked stringy, as if it needed to be washed. Her skin was pale white, almost translucent. Her eyes were

41

a faded blue.

Evelyn, he named her, was always the second in the group. She had short, curly gray hair that also looked dirty and stringy. It appeared as if something had been spilled over her head, leaving a dried brown color streaking through the curls. Her gray eyes were covered with silver-rimmed glasses that looked slightly fogged.

Annie, as he designated the third, was always the last one, lingering behind Mary and Evelyn. She was the first to duck out of sight when Edwin spotted the group, and the last one to enter his sight line when he searched for them: the followers. Annie was younger, barely into her teens.

They were three generations of the same family. Grandmother Evelyn, Mother Mary, and Granddaughter Annie.

All during Edwin's trial they had followed him, watching his every move, never saying a word.

He was surprised they didn't occupy the cell next to him, but when he thought about it, he knew they couldn't be there. The prison was for male prisoners only.

He had spoken with the prison doctor about the followers, but the subject became moot when they didn't show up for ten years. He was actually given a sentence of twenty years, but believe it or not, the governor commuted his sentence and he was released early, based on his excellent behavior in prison. The fact that their deaths were the result of an accident, not intentional, and the fact that he really did have a medical problem were the explanations used to convince the governor. He didn't even know the three people who were killed when his car plowed into them head-on.

He had been totally unconscious when it happened—a seizure, maybe—and he didn't know what had happened until he woke up in the hospital, a week later.

He didn't drink or do drugs, but the media always insinuated that he was under the influence of something. It was neither, and his blood tests had proven that fact.

All he could ever remember was that he was driving along a country road on a beautiful, sunny day... Then he woke up in the hospital.

They didn't believe him when he told them he could remember nothing about what had happened.

"I swear to God, I don't remember hitting that car. I don't remember even *seeing* the car," he explained to policemen, prosecutors, and his own attorney, knowing they all thought he was lying through his teeth.

The doctors at the prison finally saw firsthand that he had a medical problem, which caused him to pass out for no apparent reason. They advised him never to drive a car again, or operate any kind of heavy machinery that could cause harm to him or anyone in his path.

They called his brain malfunction by a long name that he could neither spell nor say. He took pills daily to prevent the so-called seizures, and when he left the prison, the doctor handed him a prescription to be filled in the outside world.

He hadn't filled the prescription yet. He had wanted to do that when he arrived home. All he wanted to do was go home, never realizing that the followers would be there until he was a few miles from his town.

Then the thought hit him.

They would be waiting for him. They would be after their pound of flesh which was him.

He lay down on the bed, hoping to fall asleep rapidly. As his eyelids started to feel heavy, Mary, Evelyn, and Annie stood around his bed, gazing at him.

The last thing that had passed through his mind before going to sleep was *I should have gotten my prescription filled.*

He never woke up in the town that he loved again, because Mary, Evelyn, and Annie had finally gotten their pound of flesh—Edwin.

THE OMEN

SUSANNA CONNELLY HOLSTEIN

Y ou ain't gonna be able to help her this time, Mother. She's real bad.
We'll have to take her over the mountain to Harrisonburg, get her
some real doctoring at the sanatorium."

Caley Parsons looked at her tall son, standing in her doorway. His
face was lined with worry, and it shook in his voice. "You know these
woods medicines, but this tuberculosis, they call it, it's really got hold of
Mandy. She's really bad sick. I need Tom and Jim to help me, go with me
right now. The roads are terrible, and they're gettin' worse. We've got to
go now."

"I understand, Bill. You got to do what you got to do. I've tried, but
Mandy is just too sick for anything I can do."

He nodded and turned away, walking quickly to the barn, where his
brothers were mending tack. The old woman sighed and turned back to
her kitchen.

She knew she had certain gifts. She could doctor people when they
were ill, and was often called on to do so by the neighbors in Pendleton
County, West Virginia. Everyone knew Granny Caley Parsons was the one
you went to if you had any kind of ailment; the woods and fields were
her medicine chest, she claimed, and people believed her. She knew what
plants would heal a sore, what to brew into a tea to calm a fever, how to
make a poultice to draw the venom out of a snakebite. But tuberculosis?

She sighed again and lifted the cloth covering the rising bread dough in the warming oven.

"Hate them boys driving all that way in this weather," she fretted wiping her hands on her apron for the tenth time. This February of 1928 was shaping up to be the coldest on record, with snowfall almost every day and temperatures sinking to zero or below night after night. Travel in such weather was a risky business, but she knew there was only one way to cure tuberculosis: go to a sanatorium. The closest one to the farm was in Virginia, a treacherous journey over Sewell Mountain on snow-covered roads. Another sigh escaped her. Nothing to do but let them go.

Caley went about her work that day, but she could not concentrate. Her sons should be home by early evening, and she would have dinner waiting for them. As she passed a window on her way upstairs, she glanced out the window.

"What..."

A large ball of fire was rolling down the creek in front of the house. She watched in amazement as it rolled along the frozen water and out of sight around a bend. How could what she was seeing be possible? She shook herself as if to shake off a bad dream, and stared at the creek. A melted track of snow lined the center of the creek, as far as she could see.

"I didn't dream that thing! I know what I saw, sure as I'm standin' here! And I know what it is, too. That's an omen, a bad one. Those boys won't be back."

Caley knew there were signs that meant trouble was roaming the land. Like hearing an owl in the daytime meant the owl was calling death to a house; others claimed a bird flying in a window meant the same thing. Caley paid little attention to most such talk, but she remembered her mother telling her of seeing a ball of fire roll across a hayfield. Soon after, her mother told her, the horses spooked at a snake and turned the hay wagon over, killing two boys. That ball of fire was an omen, her mother pronounced. That's what it was, an omen sent by the Almighty—or maybe by the Dark One. She never spoke the Dark One's name. Calling his name was just calling trouble, her mother claimed.

The back door creaked open and her husband stomped inside. He brushed snow off his shoulders and slipped off his boots onto the rug by the door.

"Are you all right, Caley?" he asked, looking at her. "You're lookin' a little pale. You're not getting sick, are you? All this tuberculosis going around..."

"I'm not sick. I'm just worried about the boys. I know they're grown men and all, but I don't like them going in this storm. Maybe they should have waited, and taken Mandy over there tomorrow."

"It's a bad day out there," Ron Parsons agreed. "I tried to talk them out of going, but they wouldn't listen. There will be a lot more snow before this storm is over. They're gonna have a time getting' back over that mountain. They'll be all right, though. They know the road."

"They won't be back," Caley said, softly to herself. "They won't be back."

"What?" Ron asked, but he was already standing at the stove, and didn't hear her whispered reply.

"They won't be back. Our boys are gone."

***

The Parsons brothers made the journey to Virginia safely. Bill registered his wife at the sanatorium, and settled her into her room.

"I'll be back to see you in a few days," he promised. "You just concentrate on getting' well, you hear? I've got to get going now." He hugged her and waved as he walked out the door. Mandy waved back weakly and sank back against the pillows, her eyes closed before he was out of sight.

As he got back in the car, Bill said, "Hey, you fellas hungry? Let's stop at the inn at the foot of the mountain for some food and drinks to warm us up. It's not going to be an easy trip home, so we might as well get ourselves set up good before we head up Sewell. Looks like the snow is lettin' up, so we can spare a little time, I think."

They left the inn a few hours later, full of good stew and good whiskey. They laughed and slapped each other on the back as they climbed into the car and started up the twisting road.

"Damn this snow!" Bill muttered, staring through a windshield that was almost iced over. He could barely see the road, but he could see the blowing snow and patches of ice.

The car battled for every foot up Sewell Mountain. Inside, the men were quiet, tense. They reached the top of the mountain and began the steep, curvy descent. All went well at first, but then the car began to slide.

"No! No! No!" Bill felt the wheel spinning under his hands as the car slid sideways over the mountain and down, down, down, rolling over and coming to rest in a laurel thicket. A cloud of snow rose into the air, then settled over the car and the still bodies of the men inside.

***

Caley turned away from the window and looked at the table. Ham, cornbread, beans, and fried apples waited in covered dishes on the dark wood boards. Coffee perked on the stove, its aroma hanging warm and strong in the air. Once again, she pushed aside the curtains and stared out into the dark, snowy night. She shook her head and muttered, "They'll not be back." She moved their supper to the warming oven of the stove and returned to her vigil at the window.

She was still there when the sun rose, bright and sharp on the crust of snow. Ron came in and pulled on his boots and coat. "You really think I need to go look for them? Maybe they just spent the night in town, Caley."

"No." Caley turned toward him and shook her head. "They're on the mountain. Please, Ron, go and get our boys." She turned back to the window.

"All right. I'll go roust up some men to help me. Keep that coffee pot warm."

It didn't take the men long to find the tracks of the wayward car. They scrambled down the side of the mountain, one yelling, "Here it is, boys! Here they are!"

He grew quiet as the other men joined him, and stared inside the battered car at the three frozen bodies piled together against the door. Ron sank into the snow, head in his hands.

"She was right, Caley was. She said they'd not be coming home."

Caley watched the somber procession pull into the yard. She sucked in a deep breath, then pushed back her shoulders and walked outside.

The men clambered out of the truck and silently began to unload their frozen cargo.

"Take them to the wood house," she called. She pulled on her coat, gloves, and boots and made her way to the wood house. She helped the men gently pack the bodies of her sons in the snow, then closed the door and led the way back to the house.

"We'll bury them when the ground thaws," Caley said. "It won't be until the laurel leafs out. That's when we'll be able to dig their graves."

She turned to look back at the creek. The ice was solid and snow-covered, and Caley felt its chill settle deep inside her as she entered the golden warmth of her kitchen.

In the spring, when the soft green leaves of the Laurel began to unfurl and the snow had left the mountains, the three brothers were buried. The ball of fire was never seen again.

FOREVER

APRIL HENSLEY

Darkness wrapped around me like a gentle cocoon, protecting me. Tucked away in a safe place of quiet and peace, I cherished these few stolen moments. It was my only time of rest, when I could drift away and forget about the rage and sorrow and longing of my soul. If only the peace would last for eternity—but it was to be only a brief remission again. Awareness was always on the edge of my consciousness. Waiting, watching, listening...always waiting. Forever waiting.

Suddenly a scalding yellow light pierced through to the very core of my soul. Ripping me out of the darkness, my outstretched hands clawed at emptiness, finding nothing to cling to. I was dumped back into a world I desperately wanted to abandon, but wasn't allowed to let go of yet.

Opening my eyes, I looked around to get my bearings. I was still on the scarred walnut staircase. Since all the furniture had been moved out again, it was the last place left to sit. Wanting to gather my thoughts, I had only planned to rest for a few minutes. I had no idea how much time had actually passed. Dust floated weightlessly in a multi-colored beam of summer sunshine. It came from the brightly patterned stained-glass window above the wide landing, where the stairs split behind me. Daddy had installed it as his wedding gift to me and Archer. Midmorning sun had spilled down the stairs into the front parlor ever since. The light shone through my hand but I felt no warmth, only bone chilling cold. The window was one

49

of the only elegant things remaining from a once well-loved farmhouse, now neglected and forgotten.

My senses tingled as I strained to hear anything in the deafening silence. Something completely different was in the air. Even the house seemed to be at attention. There it was! The distant roar of an approaching motorized vehicle echoed in the abandoned house. This back country had very little traffic. My favorite navy gingham dress made a silky whisper on the dirty hardwood floor, but my boots made no sound as I rushed across the parlor to one of the only front windows not boarded up. Anxiously I peered through the grime, hoping beyond hope to fulfill my promise. Maybe Archer would finally keep his, too. Beyond the wraparound porch with its missing spindles lay the weedy, overgrown front lawn. The giant oak tree protecting the front of the house was now a rotting stump. The heart carved into the side of the tree, announcing Archer + Elizabeth, had deteriorated and blown away years ago. A dirt road crossed in front of the property. If news were to finally come, it would be from the direction of town. As the billowing dust grew closer and closer, I felt something I hadn't felt in a long time. A tiny whimper that sounded like "please" moved the air.

A patriotic colored boxy vehicle slowed to make the sharp turn in the road just past my house. It was only the mailman. How could I have gotten so excited, when I knew the sound of his vehicle so well? The driver glanced casually towards the house and looked directly at me. Shock and terror flashed in his eyes. The noisy engine revved loudly as he sped up quickly. His tires skidded a little as he took the curve past the house a little too fast, almost flattening the faded "For Sale" sign near the road.

The wall caught me as I weakly slumped forward. A low mournful cry settled into the walls. For a moment, the constant rage had fallen away and faith had taken hold of me. My old friend grief rushed back to take its place, but I quickly pushed it aside with my bitterness. As my anger built, the rotting porch swing began to slowly sway in the still air. I stared blindly into the distance. The Blue Ridge Mountains spread low and wide on the horizon. It was the reason the Virginia town had been named Pleasant View. The beauty of it all was lost on me, as I had sadly stared at it tens of thousands of times.

It was my own fault people were afraid of me. I had heard the whispers for years. Strange, weird, crazy...evil. People fear what they don't under-stand. I never meant to scare anybody. In my own defense, I had never hurt anyone. My fury had destroyed things and uprooted people, though. Seemingly small things set me off. The bitterness I never showed in life had always been just beneath the surface. Now it came easily. Pretense no longer mattered. All that was left of me were emotions, and I had no control of them.

I hadn't always been an angry person. Laughter came easily, like gentle water rolling in the little stream out back. Every day had been a grand adventure. There was so much to do and look forward to. Ice skating on the pond and picnics, church socials, hayrides, and taking the train to Chesapeake, Virginia.

That was before the war. The townspeople and newspapers said the war would never touch us. None of the things the rich politicians fought over had anything to do with our simple way of life, here in the Appala-chian Mountains. They were wrong.

Life was a dance to fiddle music: brighter, faster, as I struggled to catch my breath. Then a dark cloud moved over our little piece of heaven. The laughter faded away to tears and stopped, as more and more horrible news filtered into town. Our lively mountain music was silenced. The inno-cence was forever gone.

Archer and I had clung to each other. "Promise me you will come home!"

"I will be here! Promise me you will wait for me."

"Forever," I swore. It was the last time I saw his face.

For years during and after the war, I watched for him on the road. When I accepted he wasn't coming home alive, I waited for his body. For years I wrote letters to congressmen and senators, and even several presi-dents. The governor of Virginia was the only one who wrote back, prom-ising to look into the matter. The rest either ignored me, or sent typed letters full of apologies and appreciation for my sacrifice. If only I could find out what happened, I felt I might finally have peace. I had waited for 67 years. Still, I waited. It looked like my promise of forever might truly last forever.

Lost in thought, I didn't notice the sounds of another vehicle ap-proaching until it was almost upon me. The vehicle completely missed the gravel driveway and jumped the small ditch, bouncing the silver automobile into the air before it came to a tooth-jarring stop inches from the porch. Instinctively, I jumped away from the window in fear.

An older, platinum blonde woman swung out of the driver's door. I recognized her immediately as Linda Roberts, the real estate agent. She had tried to sell the house for a long time, often renting it to unsuspecting people with a wish to escape city life for a taste of country living. Her name and a much younger picture of her were on the For Sale sign out front.

A tall lean man stretched out of the back, and quickly stepped forward to open the front passenger door. My hands flew to my mouth in shock. He looked so much like Archer! Dark curls tickled his collar on a pale blue button up shirt like my husband used to wear. Dark eyes illuminated his calm expression. A small brunette with a gently curving figure stepped out of the car, gripping his hand. She wore a sunflower yellow sundress with tiny white flowers that hung loosely in the front, and her long hair was pulled into a high ponytail. He tucked her hand into the crook of his arm as he swung the door closed.

On closer inspection, he didn't really look much like Archer after all. Archer was wider and stouter, more confident in his walk, like a man who knew his worth. This man seemed boyish, with smooth unlined hands. Archer's hands, even though just as young as the man outside, were already work-worn and rough. Archer wore his sleeves rolled up to his elbows and his shirt tucked neatly into his pants. The fellow outside had his sleeves buttoned at the cuff while letting his shirttails hang loose.

The real estate agent was pointing at the land across the road, where the barn sat slightly tilted, and at the cemetery, with its three anonymous sunken holes in the ground. The couple wasn't looking at what Miss Roberts was gesturing at. They motioned to the house. I stepped back from the window, hoping they didn't see me. The last owners had gone to a lot of trouble and expense to get rid of me. For their own mental well-being, I decided it was best to let them believe it had worked.

A skeleton key rattled in the double front doors, prompting me to dart to a shadowed corner behind the dining room archway. The hinges squeaked loudly, proclaiming they had not been used in a long while. Leaving the door open, all three crossed the creaking hardwood floors to the middle of the room. The couple circled in place, throwing long shadows.

They appeared in awe of the massive rock fireplace and beamed high ceilings.

The man spoke first, with a sincere gentleness in his voice. "What can you tell us about the house and property?"

Linda Roberts handed them both some papers and pointed out some places on a map. "This is the plat. Here you go, Joseph. Would you like a copy also, Grace? The land is around eighty-nine acres. I think it used to be much larger, but was sold off a little at a time. It stretches behind the house and across the road. There is a small creek in the back. As for the house, I don't really know much."

Joseph proudly chuckled as his wife sheepishly pulled a sheaf of papers out of the large leather handbag hanging from her shoulder.

"My wife is a history teacher at the middle school. She did some research on the house at the library this morning before our appointment."

"I'm addicted to history. What can I say?" Grace's pleasant laugh brightened the room.

"Here is a picture of the front of the house I found in an old book on Pleasant View." Joseph and Miss Roberts pulled in close to Grace as she displayed a number of photocopied sheets. I drifted silently over to get a look, too. "The photo was taken around nineteen fifty. You can't see much for that huge tree. The history is foggy, because a lot of records were lost during the Civil War. They think it was built in eighteen fifty-nine, for Archer Beaumont. He was the owner of the land. There was a local builder named Beaumont around that time, so he or his father may have built the house. Nobody knows for sure."

She was mostly right. Archer and his father had built it together. It was finished in late 1860, right before we wed.

"I saved the best for last. Check out this painting of Archer's wife Elizabeth. In this old sepia-tone photograph, the portrait looks like it was hanging right here over the fireplace. Isn't she stunning? I wonder if it's in a museum, or with her family."

There I was in my pink wedding dress. The brown and white photograph didn't show the dress in its full glory. It had been such a pale shade of pink satin it looked almost white. The wide hooped skirt barely showed a hint of my tiny matching pink shoes. It had been a magical dress for the best day of my life. My auburn hair was loosely pulled back into a low bun, with a white rose tucked over my ear. A bouquet of matching roses was in my hands. The artist had captured my green eyes sparkling. Daddy had thought 19 years old was too young to get married. Especially with the rumblings of war, he wanted to send me to stay with some distant family overseas. Nothing he said could sway me from making my lifelong choice.

I watched the real estate agent closely as Grace talked animatedly. Linda Roberts pretended she had never seen the picture before, but I knew she had; I'd followed her as she removed it from the attic and put it in her car. During my later years, I had decided it was too painful to look at anymore and stored it behind some broken-down furniture in a dark corner. She always pretended she couldn't see me, but I knew she could. As I glanced over her shoulder I leaned in closer, just to watch the fine hairs on the back of her neck stand straight up.

"It says that she made a lot of money selling timber off this land. It doesn't say anything else about the husband."

Joseph patted her on the shoulder jokingly. "Don't worry my dear, just another mystery for you to solve."

Linda harrumphed loudly, unimpressed. "Like I said, I don't know much about the house. You can see it's in really bad shape, so it's a good thing you're going to tear it down."

My body began to shake. The air around me started to vibrate with red waves of panic exploding from me. I closed my eyes tightly. A hard gust blew across the room, slamming shut the open front door. A loud banging came repeatedly from somewhere upstairs.

This was why I didn't want people in my house. This place was not only made of wood and nails. It was held together with love and promises. It didn't matter what happened to me. I had to do whatever necessary to make sure Archer had a place to come back home to.

Coughing from the dust stirred up, the agent scurried over to tug uselessly on the door. The couple seemed unfazed by the events. Joseph walked calmly over to help her. As he slipped past her to take over he looked puzzled. "We do not want to tear down the house. What would give you that idea? We are looking at it to renovate and live here."

My wrath stopped as suddenly as it started. The door opened easily when the man turned the knob. The banging ceased. I could hardly believe this man and woman might want to fix up my house.

"You said you are a builder." Linda paused to sneeze. "I thought you are going to build houses on the property."

Grace had crossed the room and joined them at the door. They shared a secret smile meant just for them.

"No," the woman said, "we are looking for a home to raise a family." Her hand moved absently to cradle her slightly rounded stomach. The man's eyes followed. "We really like this area, and the house is charming."

A baby! When Archer had built the house, we had made sure it was big enough for lots of children. Sadly, we hadn't been married for long when he was called up. We agreed that when he came back we would start a family. There had been other people's children living here, but no babies. Some of the children who knew I was here had been very scared of me, and that was the reason a lot of families moved out.

The young woman was bending down, examining the floor. "Look at all the little dents in the floor Joseph. What could have caused them?"

Archer and I had wanted to do something special as a thank you to all the townspeople for coming out to help build our barn. There were bright, clear stars in the sky that night; I could hear the infectious laughter, the thump of dancing feet. Heeled shoes came down faster and harder on the new hardwood floors as the music got quicker and louder, until the candle flames jumped in time with the fiddle.

Linda glared disapprovingly at the floor. "You will have to rip all these boards up and replace them. Those dents will never sand out."

Joseph smiled. "It's okay. I think it gives the room character. It is an old house, so it's going to have some dents and dings here and there. The house is remarkably sound and well built. There are a few major things to tackle, but we are up to the challenge if we decide to buy."

These people were starting to impress me.

Linda Roberts seemed intent on talking them out of the house. It was little wonder it been for sale for so long. "There's an overgrown cemetery across the road that goes with the property." She pointed to a symbol on a paper she held in her hand. "All the markers are gone or unreadable."

"Yes, I noticed the cross on the plat. If we decide to buy, we will have to see about getting it cleaned up." He looked over at Grace and she nodded in agreement.

"I would love to do some research to find out who is buried there."

Daddy had come home during the war in the back of a wagon, in a long wooden box. Momma joined him in the new burial plot not long after. Sometimes I longed to follow them to the other side. I wondered if they waited there for me. Maybe Archer was there, too. But once I had turned away from the light, I didn't know if it would ever come back for me. None of that mattered, though. The only thing that mattered was keeping my promise.

"All right. No problem with us." Joseph looked over at Linda gazing out the front door. "I think we would like to see the rest of the house now."

Linda fidgeted restlessly. "There's one more thing I think I'd better disclose. Everyone who has lived here says the house is haunted." Linda waved her hand vaguely in the air to include the whole house. The whites of her eyes were showing slightly around her irises. "People say they have heard and seen things. Scary things."

Linda appeared to be holding her breath, waiting for their answer. I felt as if I was, too.

The couple stared at each other intently for a moment and then burst into laughter. "There's no such thing as ghosts!" This seemed to make them both laugh even harder, until the wife was wiping tears away. Eventually, Linda joined in too.

"The only thing this place is haunted with is history. It's one of the reasons we love it. I can't wait to do more research into the people who lived here, and find out what happened to them."

As they all turned to make their way to the wide staircase the man gently put his hand on the small of his wife's back to let her go first. I remembered when Archer had been such a gentleman. I felt a sharp stab of jealousy. Moments like this reminded me more harshly than others how much I had lost.

My senses had warned me something was going to be different about this day. The feeling from earlier was still in the air, and it had grown more pronounced. It was barely recognizable as anticipation. If everything worked out, these folks were going to fix up my house while I waited for word of Archer. The best news was there was finally going to be a baby just for me.

Grace shivered and rubbed her arms. Her husband wrapped his arm around her shoulders. "Hey. What's wrong honey? Are you okay?" She silently nodded as she looked suspiciously back down the stairs.

I trailed discreetly behind them, watching. I liked this couple very much. It was the first time I was happy with the thought of someone else moving in. *Yes, I think it would be great for them to live here. With me.*

WHITE HART

DANA K. ALLEN

Lemuel Sanford turned the black mule that inspired his nickname toward home, leading a sleek pack mule and a string of sad-looking animals. There were broken-down mules, spavined horses, and a few limping ponies hobbling along on rotted or split hooves. None of the animals was sound, but by the time he worked on them a bit, all would look like prize equines to their buyers.

Lemuel was a farrier, and a good one. He had to ride circuit to serve his far-flung customers, carrying his small anvil, hoof nippers, rasps, and iron shoes on his pack mule, Lilith. Along the way, he bought unwanted animals for a song and made them shine again—long enough to sell them for a nice profit, at least. To keep his gains, it paid to be a good shot with a good gun, like the new Winchester rifle in its holster in front of his saddle. Robbers could pop out of any bush in the harsh year of 1916.

As he rode past the ramshackle sheds of the general store, Ben Bibbee hailed him from the front porch of the nearest shack. "Hey, Black Jack! You got a herd of thoroughbreds there!"

"They don't look like much now, but they'll clean up fine."

"I'm sure they will. Nobody copes horseflesh like you. When you goin' to trim Tony's hooves and reshoe him?"

"Bring him by my place tomorrow. I'm too tired tonight."

"Tomorrow's Sunday."

"And you got too much religion to get your horse's feet fixed on the Lord's day."

"'On the seventh day, He rested,'" replied Ben.

"When I make a world, I'll take a day off, too." Lemuel raised his chin in a goodbye gesture.

"There's a turkey shoot tomorrow after church. You gonna show up?"

"Don't I always?" He kicked his riding mule Job in the ribs, prompting him down the dusty road. *Now there's a religion as makes sense. Shoeing a horse on Sunday is a sin, and blowing the head off a turkey ain't.*

His youngest children—Jacob, Reva, Annabella, and Cleeve—saw him coming and ran to meet him at the gate. They herded his purchases into the field, chattering about the animals' various faults and how Poppa would fix them.

His eldest, Regina, hung out their meager wash while the next two, both boys, lounged on the porch. James' harmonica played a quiet melody over the chords from Thomas' dulcimer. As Lemuel whoaed his beasts in front of the house, they hailed him with, "Hey, Poppa!"

"Hey, boys. Y'all jump up, now. Unsaddle Job and unpack Lilith, then help the little 'uns with the rest."

They scrambled to do his bidding.

He went inside and washed the road dust from his face, then went out back to greet Regina. Since her mama died four years before, when Cleeve was born, Regina had been the woman of the house. He laid a brief hand on her arm.

She favored him with a critical eye cast over her shoulder, looking for signs of drink. "The road been kind to ya, Poppa?" she asked.

"We'll get by."

"That's good. Bella's growin' so fast I can barely keep her bottom covered." She finished hanging the laundry, picked up her empty willow basket and headed to the house. "It's time for her schooling. The last bag of flour has mealybugs. I sifted them out, but they musta been there a while, 'cause it sure don't taste good."

He smiled into her complaints. "We've got enough for clothes and white flour both."

She smiled back. "I've got leather britches on the stove. I'm about to whip up some cornbread, and Jim might get us a rabbit."

"How 'bout some fried chicken?"

"We barely got enough hens for eggs. Fox's been gettin' them. The boys take turns watchin', but so far they're just wastin' time and bullets. They haven't brought in many rabbits, either."

"Guess it's time to align the sights again on that old rifle." He paused. "Been hard, hey Girl?"

"The usual things, just more of 'em."

Lemuel made a brief trip to the orchard with his gun and came back with two large but lean conies. He skinned and gutted them, gave them to Regina for cooking, then salted and stretched the skins and hung them on the south wall of the house to dry.

That evening they feasted on fried rabbit, cornbread, and the green beans. Then they opened up the packages he'd bought down in Bluefield.

Lemuel chuckled at the surprise in Regina's eyes when she pulled out yards and yards of calico, muslin, and denim. And there were new shoes for everyone. "See, I remembered school."

In the contented silence, James spoke. "Poppa, what do you think of the war?"

"I think the war is no concern of ours. One of the few things I thank God for is that you and Thomas are too young for that nonsense. Let's fix our own problems before we take on other people's."

This was the expected response, but that didn't stop Jim. "Poppa, I'm fifteen years old and a man..."

"You're fifteen years old, and a boy who's a bit thick between the ears sometimes."

"I'm old enough to grow a beard and take your place here when you're gone."

Lemuel's face darkened with the look he got when very angry. "I can get that peach fuzz off your face with soap, water, and elbow grease. And as for being in charge when I'm gone, all of you listen to Regina and mind her good!" Then his manner softened. "Good God, boy! You've been tryin' for two weeks to snuff a defenseless little fox. What you gonna do when somethin' shoots back?"

James stalked out into the twilight in silence.

When night came, Black Jack himself sat up to meet the fox. In the morning, there was a fire-red pelt beside the rabbits'.

He slept late next morning, with all the children off down the mountain to the church and the house quiet. At least he thought all of them were off down the mountain, until Jake ran into the room whispering loud enough to rattle the windows. "Pa! Pa! Get up! Pa, it's ole Whitmore, the Witch Man. He wants to see you."

Lemuel rolled to the edge of the bed and pulled on his pants and boots.

"Don't go down there, Poppa!"

"Well, he walked all the way from Matoaka. I'd better see what he wants."

"Whatever he wants, it's bound to be evil."

"If I see harm in it, I won't do it." He clomped off down the stairs and made a stand on the porch, his wiry arms and chest bare to the dog-day sun. "Hey, Mr. Whitmore. What can I do you for?" He grinned his customer grin and waited.

Whitmore was a squat man, a white man by all accounts, but as brown as saddle leather. He had a shock of straight hair so white you could see it for a mile on a moonless night. He looked right through Lemuel's charm. "Well, Black Jack Sanford. I was hopin' you'd do some smithin' for me."

Lemuel disliked the sound of his name in this man's mouth, even his nickname, but not liking someone never stopped him from making money. "Y'all got a real smithy over to Matoaka. What you comin' all this way for?"

"The smith, Red Cadle, don't like me much. You want the job or not?"

"I'll help you out if I can, but mostly I just shape horseshoes and straighten bent tools and such. What do you want?"

"Well, I need a big iron collar, about this size." Whitmore held his hands up to indicate.

"It'd take a bear to fill up that collar."

Whitmore said nothing.

"Well, like I said, I'm no great shakes as a smith." He thought a minute and came up with a reasonable sum for the service.

Seemingly from the empty air behind his back, Whitmore pulled out a short bar of iron. "What if I brought my own metal?"

Lemuel wiped the puzzled look off his face and said, "Well, most of the cost is in the labor, but it'll save you a penny or two."

"That's still a steep price, but I got no choice." The old man reached behind himself and pulled out a page of rolled-up parchment. He handed it to Lemuel, saying, "This here's it."

Jake assessed the drawing on the scroll and realized he had seriously underpriced the job. *Well, a deal is a deal,* he rationalized grimly.

Whitmore wandered over by the fence and watched the herd run skittishly up and down the far side of the field.

As Lemuel pondered how to proceed, he noticed the brown color of the ink and the strange texture of the parchment. He'd seen a lot of real parchment, but whatever animal this skin came from was new to him. And did that look like stitches across that scar? *This is some trick to rattle me,* he thought, but his hands shook regardless. He put the drawing down and began to work.

The collar curved like a snake and hinged with two entwined loops in back, coming together in the front with a clasp like two lizard's claws clamped together, one in front of the other. Lemuel finished shaping the metal, picked it up with tongs, and quenched it in a bucket of spring water. He rasped off some sharp edges, then gave it a good coat of blacking so it wouldn't rust. He turned around to call Whitmore, but the old man was right there. As the blacking hadn't completely cured, he held the collar out with tongs so that Whitmore could examine his work.

"That's a fine job," said Whitmore, smiling. He reached for the collar.

"I'll take my pay now, if you please."

"Certainly, certainly. But I was hopin' you might like a trade."

His curiosity piqued, Lemuel asked, "What kind of trade?"

"Well, I could fix that scroungy herd you have with a little chant." He looked at Lemuel as if the farrier had better take his offer.

"I can fix that herd myself, and without no chantin', neither. You better find something more interestin' to trade, or cash money."

"I don't have no truck with money," said Whitmore. Something flashed in his hand. "Will you take gold?"

"If it's real gold, and if it's enough to pay for my time."

"It is. More than enough."

"Let's see it."

"One last thing. Put this little design on the clasp."

"What design?"

"This," said Whitmore, holding his hand open more to show a golden circle with a five-pointed star inside it.

In for a penny, in for a pound, thought Lemuel. He took the little pentacle and with one heavy stroke of his hammer, cold welded it to the clasp.

"Here's your gold," said Whitmore. He held out a pentacle just like the one on the collar.

The gold in the charm was worth ten times his day's labor, so Lemuel swallowed his misgivings and took it.

Old Man Whitmore strolled back down the gravel road, whistling a dirge like a dance tune.

Lemuel took his hammer and pounded the charm until it was unrecognizable, then folded it with pliers and pounded it again. This he repeated until his arms shook from strain, not from fear. Finally, he took the lump of gold down to the creek and hid it under a green rock, planning to leave it there until the dark of the moon, when all the evil would be washed away.

With less enthusiasm than a turkey shoot usually raised, Lemuel rode Job, the black mule, down to the general store. He took Jacob with him, carrying his old gun, riding on Lilith. As usual, Lemuel shot both birds in the turkey shoot, right through the eyes.

Jacob gave a good account at the boys' target shoot, winning a small pocket knife for himself and a pencil box for Annabella. Lemuel and Jacob left the match to buy a wedge of cheese, a huge dill pickle, and some crackers for their lunch. They sat in the shade of a big willow tree to eat, and washed it down with spring water.

"That Witch Man ain't natural."

"What's unnatural about him?" asked Lemuel, although he thought he knew. That man didn't feel right.

"Well, he's renounced God, and he's supposed to be able to do all kinds of black magic."

"Jacob, I've told you a hundred times not to start up that trash novel nonsense with me."

"Your boy is right," said Ben Bibbee as he strode up on his long legs. "That Witch Man has broke with God, dippin' himself in a creek on a full moon and reciting, 'I renounce thee God,' seven times. Then Old Scratch showed up and gave him the power."

"How do you know so much about it, Ben?"

"Well, he tells anyone who sits long enough to listen, like he was proud of it."

"Or just havin' fun spookin' you."

Offended, Ben made his lanky way back toward the cool, dark interior of the store. "You'll see, you mule-headed shit shoveler. You'll see."

"And I reckon you can find someone else to shoe Tony," Lemuel said and went back to eating.

As if summoned, Whitmore stood in front of them. He had Lemuel's rifle in his hands. "You've done well with your new rifle. You're the finest shot around, a very deadly man," he said.

Lemuel just stared at him.

"Black Jack, my friend, I just want to ask you a favor." He pushed on before the farrier could protest. "When you and your sons go hunting, will you spare any white animals you find?"

Lemuel rose to face the old man. "First off, I ain't your friend. Second, if you have special critters you don't want shot, you keep them penned up. Times are lean, and one meal might make the difference for me and mine, come a bad winter."

As Lemuel said this, Whitmore's face darkened and clouded over. Then he smiled. He moved his hands up and down the barrel of Black Jack's gun.

"And finally," said Lemuel, snatching his rifle from the white-haired man, "I don't like people handling my gun without askin'." He put his palm in the middle of Jacob's back and propelled him toward the match. "It's time to shoot again."

Lemuel made a sorry sight in the target matches. Even though he had checked the sights before going out after the fox, all his shots went wide by far, and never in the same direction twice. Always just in the corner of his vision, there stood Whitmore, laughing at each miss. Finally, Lemuel gave up and sought the shade of the willow. Jacob sat down beside him. They watched the Witch Man leave, waiting until he was out of sight, then headed back to the match. Lemuel tried again, without success. Then they left, too.

Firing his Winchester over and over at the knot in the locust post brought no relief from frustration, so Lemuel made himself an angry pendulum on the porch swing. Jacob came up and sat down by his father, commiserating.

"I hate to admit it, but I think I got witched." Lemuel grinned ruefully at his son.

"Pa, try your old gun. He didn't touch it."

Lemuel aimed with the Browning rifle and plugged the hole on the first shot. "It's not me. It's the gun."

"Let me try it," said Jake.

Lemuel hesitated.

"Pa, I bet his revenge is pointed square at you and nobody else." He took the gun. The boy aimed and shot. They could see the bark fly off the impact site, just about two inches from the knothole. He took another shot, with about the same results. "Pa, that's about as good as I ever do."

"Guess I get the Browning. Damn. That Winchester was a sweet gun."

The next morning, James was gone; the gold disappeared along with him. He left a note saying he was sorry for stealing, and that he was going to lie about his age and go off to war. Lemuel threw the note in the cookstove and watched it burn.

Autumn fell well and truly on the mountain, with days cool enough for meat to cure and nights above freezing. So Lemuel on Job, and Thomas and Jacob on Lilith, rode into the crackling oak leaves to hunt. They hid at every favorite hunting site to wait, with no luck but bad. After two weeks, the weather turned unseasonably cold and clouded up for snow. Plus, their camp supplies were too low. They headed home. Out on a ridge, they picked up freshly made deer tracks—big ones. They came up on Red Cadle and his boy Roger; the Cadles had found the tracks, too. They followed them together.

The wind picked up, and tiny ice crystals stung their faces. They gathered together, deciding once again to head for home. The cold breeze died and the sun came out. Shining in the clearing ahead was a solid white, twenty-four-point buck.

Red squeezed off a shot and missed by a mile. So did Roger and Jake. Lemuel climbed on Job and kicked him into a slow but reckless gallop through the rough terrain, following the fleeing deer. He lost sight of it, then lost the tracks. Suddenly, the buck flushed out of a clump of bushes ahead of him, but Job reared, ruining his aim.

The deer stopped just at the edge of the old Browning rifle's range, flanks heaving, red tongue hanging out, his breath like smoke in the crisp air. Lemuel raised the barrel of his gun higher to cover the distance and fired. The stag jumped, and a bloody flower bloomed from his right side. The animal looked up to the sky. The clouds gathered darkly, dropping large flakes of snow, and the deer took labored bounds along the ridge line.

Got to get him before snow covers his tracks, thought Lemuel. He grabbed for Job's reins, but the mule shied away. He set off on foot, scrabbling fast as he could to follow. Thomas, Jacob, Red, and Roger came up to Job, but their mounts moved no farther than Job had and wound up tied alongside him. The hunters followed the tracks and blood on foot.

"You know," Red informed as he caught up to Lemuel, "the Witch Man's shack is on this ridge."

A chill that had nothing to do with weather touched the pit of Lemuel's stomach.

Once, they caught up with the deer enough to see him through the snow. He was bleeding from the wound and his mouth, his breath coming out in red froth. Then he bounded away again, ever toward Whitmore's home.

"That deer looked like he had a black mark around his throat!" said Roger.

"Looked like a black snake, to me," said the smith.

The chill touched Lemuel again.

They followed the trail right up to the gate of old Whitmore's yard. The tracks stopped at the fence, but blood dripped down the gate. No deer tracks were visible on the other side of the fence—just bare, bloody, human footprints. Whitmore's front door hung open like a slack mouth.

"Halloo the house!" called Lemuel. When there was no answer, he pushed open the door with the barrel of his gun. Lying dead on the floor was Jude Whitmore, a hole in his right lung. He was naked, except for a black iron collar with a pentagram burned into the gray metal beneath the blacking.

"Better fetch Sheriff Deskins, Pa," said Jacob.

After lengthy questioning in which all witnesses held to their stories, the sheriff ruled Whitmore's death a hunting accident, albeit a suspicious one.

Lemuel came home to a surprise. A sergeant on his charger led a sullen James home on a scrawny mule. "Hello, Mr. Sanford. I'm Sergeant Williams, from Lexington. I'm here to return your overly patriotic young son."

"Much obliged," said Lemuel. "That's fine horseflesh you're riding..."

"Poppa, someone stole the gold..."

"Yes, starting with you. Climb off that critter. There's five cords of wood that needs splitting."

James ran to his punishment, puzzled that his father hadn't used the razor strop on him.

Lemuel said to the sergeant, "Come on inside for rest and a meal. Tom will see to your animals. Cold spring water, milk, or a bit of whiskey will wash away road dust, and Regina here does some fine fried chicken." Regina took notice and ran to find two pullets for the skillet.

As Lemuel ushered his guest into the house, he said, "Sergeant Williams, your mule has a limp I can fix. I'm a farrier."

"Ah. The kindest thing to do with that beast is put a bullet in its head. I see that you have a fine herd. The Army can use good animals."

Lemuel grinned his widest and said, "I'm sure we can make a deal..."

ABOUT THE AUTHORS

JAN HOWERY
"THE DEVIL BEHIND THE BARN"

Jan Howery, a native of Southwest Virginia, writes with an Appalachian influence. Her many writings include a short story, "The Daisy Flower Garden," featured in the book *Broken Petals*. Other writings include fashion and health columns for the magazines, *Voice Magazine for Women* and *Modern Day Appalachian Woman* magazine.

KATIE MEADE
"ESTHER ON YOUR BACK"

Katie Meade, a graduate from the University of Virginia and Morehead State University, has been writing and keeping journals for decades.

Her most recent work is *Just a Good Story*. Other books include *A Man Called Hatchet Jack*, *The Rainbow Ghosts*, and *Chucky the Chocolate Mouse*, which are children's book. *Stories from a Coal Camp: A Place of Yesterday* is among the author's published books for adults. Katie lives in Virginia with her husband Jack and dog Abby.

BEV FREEMAN
"HISTORY LESSON"

Bev Freeman was born in Virginia and lived in the Appalachians until her teens. Her family relocated to Florida where she graduated high school, married a Floridian, and raised a son.

In 1993, with shattered dreams, she returned to the Appalachian region. She married a local, God-fearing man in 1996, and life is beautiful in Tennessee, with two spirited grandsons living close by.

She is the author of *Silence of the Bones* and is member of The Lost State Writers Guild.

SHARYN MARTIN
"OBED'S CURSE"

Sharyn Martin is a local writer. Her writings have published in the literary journal of UVA/Wise, the "Jimson Weed." She has also won short story and essay competitions published in 'Explorations', an online art and literary journal of Mountain Empire Community College, as well as winning the adult non-fiction writing contest for the Appalachian Heritage Writers Symposium. She has also won short story competition in the Lonesome Pine Short Story Contest.

LINDA HUDSON HOAGLAND
"ONLY TIME WILL TELL" AND "THE FOLLOWERS"

Linda Hudson Hoagland has won acclaim for her 13 mystery novels that include the recent *Onward & Upward, Missing Sammy,* and *Snooping Can Helpful–Sometimes.* She is also the author of 8 works of nonfiction, 2 collections of short writings along with 2 volumes of poems. Her work has appeared in many anthologies.

Hoagland taught creative writing classes for the College for Older Adults on the Virginia Highlands Community Campus at the Higher Ed Center, Abingdon, Virginia, in 2015, 2016, and 2017.

Linda Hudson Hoagland is former President of the Appalachian

Authors Guild (2015) and a member of the Advisory Board for the Humanities at Bluefield State College.

WILLIE E. DALTON
"SO THEY SAY..."

Willie E. Dalton grew up in the tiny town of Pound, Virginia. Even from a small age she was drawn to things ignored by most kids. Her favorite past time was pretending to be a fairy or a gypsy fortune teller draped in scarves, using an old globe from a light fixture as her crystal ball.

After several years working in holistic health she decided to turn to her passion of writing full-time. Her first novel *Three Witches in a Small Town* was the winner of the 2015 Jan Carol Publishing Believe and Achieve Award. Since then, she's written another full length novel and has had a few short stories and poems published in literary journals and anthologies.

Please follow Willie on the websites below to stay up to date on future works: www.threewitchesinasmalltown.wordpress.com, www.authorwilliedalton.com, www.facebook.com/threewitchesinasmalltown, and on Twitter @willieedalton.

SUSANNA CONNELLY HOLSTEIN
"THE OMEN"

Susanna Holstein maintains and writes for her blog, *Storyteller Granny Sue: Stories from the Mountains and Beyond*. Her poetry, nonfiction and fiction works have won numerous awards at the WV Writers Annual Conference.

Holstein also writes an online journal, *Granny Sue's News and Reviews*, the poetry blog *Mountain Poet*, and a monthly column for the central West Virginia publication *Two Lane Livin'*. Her work has appeared in two anthologies of stories about Appalachian women, as well as in other print and online journals. When not writing, researching or telling stories, she enjoys gardening, canning, and a country lifestyle on her small farm in Jackson County. Contact her at: susannaholstein@yahoo.com. Visit her on the web at: www.grannysu.blogspot.com, www.grannysue.blogspot.com, www.mountainpoet.wordpress.com, www.twolanelivin.com, and www.facebookcom/grannysu.

April Hensley
"Forever"

April Hensley's favorite memories of childhood are of exploring the woods, wildlife and waters of the Appalachian Mountains. She now spends much of her free time gardening and enjoying nature. April was published in *Self Rising Flowers* writing under her pen name Maggie Thomas, and under her own name in the Jan-Carol Publishing title, *Broken Petals*. She has written for online publications and is a guest contributor to *Voice Magazine for Women*. April lives in East Tennessee with her husband and beloved fur-babies. You may reach April on Facebook at *April's Happy Blooms*.

Dana K. Allen
"White Hart"

A West Virginia resident nearly all her life, Dana K. Allen is the granddaughter of a miner on one side and a railroad worker on the other. Her whole family regaled her with stories of these weird, supernatural Appalachians. Retired to these mountains, she writes, spoils her pets, and enjoys the woods.

**Jan-Carol
Publishing, Inc**

"every story needs a book"

**LITTLE CREEK BOOKS
MOUNTAIN GIRL PRESS
EXPRESS EDITIONS
DIGISTYLE
ROSEHEART
BROKEN CROW RIDGE**

JANCAROLPUBLISHING.COM